DIAF

OF A

CZAR

VINNIE'S ODYSSEY

Diary of a Czar:
Vinnie's Odyssey
by Stephen Lytton

© Stephen Lytton
Illustrated by Gillian Lock

ISBN: 9781912092031
First published in 2022

Published by Palavro, an imprint of
the Arkbound Foundation (Publishers)

Arkbound is a social enterprise that aims to promote social inclusion, community development and artistic talent. It sponsors publications by disadvantaged authors and covers issues that engage wider social concerns. Arkbound fully embraces sustainability and environmental protection. It endeavours to use material that is renewable, recyclable or sourced from sustainable forest.

Arkbound, Rogart Street Campus
4 Rogart Street, Glasgow, G40 2AA
www.arkbound.com

DIARY

OF A

CZAR

VINNIE'S ODYSSEY

STEPHEN LYTTON

palavro
PUBLISHING

Happy Reading! Czar and Stephen.

Thank you for buying VinniesOdyssey.
Sales will be going towards opening
a Home for dogs and Animals.

This book is dedicated to Natasha, Ellie, Isla and Amy

Enjoy the illustrations.
Gillian
x

Running, running - the long grass whips my chest and flanks, all my senses alive. I stop to look around and see a movement down by the silver stream. Why, it's another Vizsla dog! I give chase. He looks up and spots me, gallops away, then, in one bound, jumps across the stream.

I follow, leaping over the tall bulrushes. Now on his tail, I can hear his panting breath. He is heading towards Acorn Wood. Before going in, he turns to face me. Growling, our heads down, we circle, sizing each other up as one, leaping up and smashing into each other to play fight, rolling around happily in the dust. He sits on me; I kick his broad chest. We jump up, bound towards each other, skidding to a halt to touch noses. He has a big happy smile on his ginger face.

"Hello my friend, I'm Vinnie. I know who you are. You're Czar, but after that friendly welcome, I shall call you Tovarisch. I'm here for my holiday." We bump chests happily.

"Vinnie, that's brilliant; you're most welcome!" We have a happy neck-to-neck nuzzle.

"So, Tovarisch, I have seen the silver stream and the pony's paddock. Please show me around the rest of your home."

Side by side, I lead my new friend into the old oak trees. "This is Acorn Wood, where the pesky squirrels live."

"Squirrels, Tovarisch? Squirrels?"

Vinnie becomes suddenly alert, as we hide behind the trunk of an old, gnarled yew. A fallen branch conceals our presence. Looking around, nothing moves - all is still - then, high up in the canopy of an ancient oak, we spy a squirrel sitting on a branch. Carefully it makes its way down the trunk to sit on a root. In his excitement, Vinnie can't contain himself. He rushes forward. "No, Vinnie!" I bark. The squirrel is far too quick and disappears around the oak. Vinnie crashes headlong into the tree, hitting his head with a thud. I shake my head. "Too fast, Vinnie!"

"Not fast enough, Tovarisch!"

Laughing, we make our way through the paddock past the two sleepy ponies, and they look up to study us with bemused expressions, before going back to pulling lazily at the grass.

We trot side-by-side back towards the silver stream. Vinnie notices a wall of pink and purple flowers. "What plant is that, Tovarisch?"

"It's called Himalayan Balsam. You must be careful, Vinnie. It attacks an unwary hound."

"A plant that attacks? What nonsense!" Vinnie strolls up to the balsam and pushes between the stalks. Instantly the green balsam seed pods explode, shooting out their tiny black seeds, stinging every part of Vinnie's body. He dashes forward, barking in alarm, which causes a chain reaction setting off more seed pods. I hear a loud splash and smile, realising he has dived into the mill pond to escape the balsam.

Climbing out, Vinnie shakes off the water and looks back at the still popping Balsam with new-found respect. "Not my finest moment, Tovarisch."

"Vinnie, my friend," I laugh, "you're as daft as a brush!"

Together we lie curled up on the grass, silently looking at the clouds. "Tovarisch, those clouds always reminds me of my home back in the Siberian Taiga forest."

"I've never heard of Siberia, Vinnie. Where is it?"

"Siberia is part of my homeland, of Mother Russia. It's a huge wilderness. The summers are sticky and hot; the winters so cold you can't feel your paws, but you get used to the heat and cold. In the winter, we wear warm coats to keep out the wind's icy blasts. The Taiga Forest is full of wild animals: deer, chipmunks, raccoon dogs, wolves, bears and the magnificent tiger."

"Tigers? You've actually seen a tiger, Vinnie?"

"Yes, Tovarisch; I was lucky enough to see the tiger three times. The Siberian tiger is a rare beast hunted by cruel poachers almost to extinction; the evil hunters grind up the tiger's bones to make magic medicine that cures nothing. Nothing, Tovarisch! Their bones are sold to rich, stupid people for more than the price of gold."

"Vinnie, that's terrible men can be so cruel to such a wondrous wild animal!"

"Tovarisch, there is no end to some men's cruelty to animals. In my life, I have experienced humans at their best and their worst. At their best, a human's love for animals is boundless; at worst, well, I have already mentioned their cruelty to the magnificent tiger."

"Would you please tell me the story of your life in the Siberian Taiga Forest, your encounters with the tiger, and how you ended up living in England?"

Vinnie sighed. "Close your eyes. I shall take you back to another time, in another world. I'm an old hound now, nearly fourteen years ..."

"Sorry, Vinnie, but before you begin, why do you call me Tovarisch?"

"Say it like this: Tove-ah-risch."

"Tove-ah-risch."

"Again, please."

"Tove-ah-risch."

"That's it! Good, Tovarisch, you have it."

"But Vinnie, what does it mean?"

"Well, it simply means comrade or friend in Russian, and I know we will be the best of friends."

Vinnie sat up and began the story of his life.

"I was born nearly five thousand miles from England in a village near the city of Omsk. My brother Istvan and I went to live in the Taiga Forest with the Cossacks, who are a proud people who love their horses. We were to join their growing pack of Vizsla hounds. My Cossack master was called Valentin."

"Vinnie?"

"Yes, Tovarisch?"

"What about the tiger?"

"My dear Czar, you have the patience of a puppy! Very well, I'll tell you first about the tiger; it's as good a place as any to start my story.

The first time I encountered the Czar of the Taiga was one evening deep in the forest near a bottomless swamp. The horses, humans and hounds were all being attacked by swarms of mosquitoes biting the soft inside of our ears, their high-pitched whine driving us all mad.

My brother Istvan, who was the pack's watcher (which was a position of great responsibility) suddenly stopped. He barked towards a thicket of larch trees nervously. Igor, our pack leader, barked for the hounds to back off. The pack took flight, panicking the horses. They reared and bucked, trying to unseat their riders, galloping headlong into the valley, but my eyes fixed on where Istvan was barking.

Then, from out of the larch pine, came the Czar of the Taiga. His black and orange stripes glowed in the setting sun, whilst one of his ears was ripped from a previous fight with a rival. He stared at me hungrily. Crouching down, he snarled - so I growled and faced him down. His ears pricked,

almost seeming amused by this cheeky orange hound - then he opened his huge mouth to roar, revealing a glistening row of sharp white teeth. Behind, I heard the hooves of a galloping horse, with Valentin – leader of the Cossack's – riding atop. He held a fiery torch in his hand, which he waved furiously at the tiger. His brave but frightened horse, Spartak, reared up, front legs flailing in the air. With a roar and a hiss, the tiger backed away, turned, and slipped back into the forest.

Once the danger had passed, the pack re-joined us. Igor, who was very angry with me for disobeying his command, bit me hard. Instead of submitting and taking my punishment, I rounded on him. We fought, our chests clashing; tearing into each other with white teeth bared; biting, thrashing, and rolling about. I pounced on him, holding him down. I had the spirit of the tiger running through me. He struggled, kicking my chest, but I didn't let him up. Eventually, Igor submitted. Defeated, he limped away. The pack surrounded me baying: 'Vinnie, Vinnie! The invincible Tiger Hound.'

In defeating Igor, I became the pack leader. That night I took his place by the fire, its warmth soothing Igor's bites. My torn ear throbbed painfully. Looking into the fire's warming flames, something didn't feel right. My victory felt hollow, and I felt guilty. I had to find Igor to make my peace.

He was out at the edge of the pack shivering in the cold. When he saw me, he slowly sat up and growled. 'You fought well, comrade.' Igor had never called me comrade before, only 'that young cur!' I asked him to join me at the fireside, and, to my joy, he agreed. Together we hobbled back to the fire, only to find it had been stolen by a clever young bitch called Catherine, who snarled at us in defiance before resentfully retreating.

Does my stand against the tiger and victory over Igor impress you, Tovarisch? Well, it shouldn't do. In my mind, I had stolen Igor's crown, but you know, Tovarisch, sometimes the worst of enemies can become the best of friends. Igor became like my second brother." Vinnie put his paw around my shoulder. "And you, Tovarisch, shall be my third!

DIARY OF A CZAR: VINNIE'S ODYSSEY

My Cossack family had two camps: the summer and, further north, the winter camp. Igor now ran the summer camp and I the winter. Moving between the two, I followed Valentin, both a master and a friend. At my side ran Igor's two tough young sons, Oleg and Pavel. Together our little band roamed all over the Taiga in search of precious amber, which Valentin would use for trading.

One frosty morning, a Cossack rider galloped into the winter camp. It was Borislav, the camp's healer. 'Vinnie, come.' He had a twinkle in his eye as he went down on his knees to give me a lovely pat. Getting up, Borislav opened his welcoming arms, giving his old friends Valentin and Mishka big bear hugs. I watched them talking happily, pointing at me. They tacked up their horses. Mounting up, they shouted, 'Vinnie, Oleg, Pavel come! On to the Summer camp!' With me leading, we all ran excitedly into the forest. Valentin decided to take a shortcut over a steep hill down into the thickly wooded valley beyond.

Night fell, bringing heavy snow. As the path through the woods began to disappear, Valentin lost his bearings. The stars he used to navigate were hidden behind black clouds. With a fire brand, Mishka lit homemade fire torches, revealing the old traders' track coming out onto a wide, newly cut road through the virgin forest. Trotting up the muddy, rutted road, I sensed something was wrong. Through the trees, I saw the flicker of approaching headlights. I barked in warning. Valentin ordered us into the safety of a passing point, and we followed hastily. Rarely had the horses seen a car - let alone a roaring, snorting truck. In vain, Valentin urged his horse to move. The truck, heavily laden with larch logs, bore down on horse and rider, blowing its horn, terrifying Valentin's horse even further. Valentin hung onto his neck, dropping his fire torch. It landed in the dirty snow, fizzing out; Valentin's hat flew off his head, also landing in the mud. Again, the truck blew its horn. The driver desperately stamped on the brakes as the truck lurched from side to side. Valentin jumped off and tried to drag the horse, imploring him to move, all to no avail. But then, as if stung by a hornet, the horse suddenly leapt forward, knocking Valentin clean off his feet. Immediately the truck roared past in a cloud of choking diesel fumes, its tyres splashing us with slushy mud. We all watched the red brake lights disappear into the falling snow.

Gingerly, I sniffed along the road until I found Valentin's crushed hat and brought it back to him. Misha laughed as muddy water dripped into Valentin's beard. Like all Cossacks, Valentin was quick to anger. Eyes full of fire, he rose up to his full height as Mishka stammered an apology. After a long moment, Valentin's mud-stained face broke out into a broad smile. The two men hugged in sweet relief. Valentin and Mishka didn't mount up; instead, they led Kira and Spartak by the light of Mishka's single torch. Warily, we made our way up the rutted road. A few miles further on, we found our path back into our Taiga - the only world we really knew and understood.

Istvan and Igor greeted us at summer camp the following day. Igor's sons jumped up, with enthusiasm before shooting off to play like puppies with their friends. Igor shook himself off, thanked me for looking after his boys, then gave me a nudge and a wink.

'There's a lovely surprise waiting for you, comrade.'

Valentin led us to an old caravan. There, in the flame light of a torch, was Catherine. The previous winter Catherine and I had become very close at Christmas. This is a festival that the Cossacks celebrate royally. In the light of the fire I asked Catherine to be my consort, and to my joy she agreed. She had now presented me with three wriggling puppies! I lay down with her and nuzzled her ear, while she gave me a tired smile.

The pups eyed me with interest, a new victim for their attentions. They leapt on me, chasing my wagging tail, nibbling my ears with their pin-sharp teeth, but I didn't care a jot. My own pups, Tovarisch! A gift, the miracle of life. I felt so proud of my lovely Catherine.

Valentin picked up two of the biggest pups. Holding them up, he said to me: 'I name these pups Ivan and Peter, after the two great Czars.' Picking up a smaller pup, he paused. 'Vinnie, this one your daughter, who I name Anastasia, after Czar Ivan the Terrible's wife. These three pups will be the future of our pack.'

Valentin knelt, bowed his head to pray, then crossed himself in the Russian Orthodox fashion. He went to the caravan door and called the assembled men and women to light a bonfire; it was time to dance and celebrate. The Cossacks love a party; any excuse to celebrate really, but a father coming home to see his brood of healthy golden-red puppies for the first time - well, that was something special."

"How marvellous for you Vinnie! It really doesn't seem so long ago I was just a pup myself. What happened to them?"

"Well, Tovarisch, the pups travelled to other packs in Siberia, keeping the Vizsla bloodline varied but pure. Every now and again, travelling around the vast Taiga, I would see them and recognise myself in their handsome faces.

I spent the following spring with Catherine and the puppies, watching them run rings around Igor, who was now their teacher. One morning, Valentin shouted for me to come. There had been rumours of tiger poachers in the hills far to the north. I rounded up the pack, while the senior Cossacks grimly loaded their rifles, revolvers and belted on their sabre swords.

Valentin led his Cossack brothers forward, following the copper green river north, crossing a vast plain towards the distant hills. We hounds ran beside the horses, day and night, matching their slow canter up rolling hills and down curving valleys.

On the third morning, racing up a steep incline to a clearing at the top, Valentin ordered me to scout on ahead. Stopping to smell the air, I caught the faint whiff of diesel fumes. I barked for the rest of the hounds to join me, our noses to the ground, with me leading the pack. I followed the scent towards a high plateau. Mishka took out his binoculars, scanned the horizon, and pointed into the distance. Our sharp eyes could just make out three trucks. Valentin drew his sabre, as all the other men followed his example. He ordered Mishka, Borislav and half of the party to track left to cut off, then envelop, the poachers – allowing none to escape. My brother took the lead, with Igor following up in the rear.

ANASTASIA
WIFE OF IVAN THE TERRIBLE

IVAN THE TERRIBLE

PETER THE GREAT

CATHERINE THE GREAT

After waiting a few seconds, with grim resolve, Valentin looked up to the heavens, said a little prayer, and ordered me to move out. Proudly, I led the way. As we neared the poachers' position, the men urged their horses into a gallop, moving forward in their saddles over their steeds flying manes, pointing glinting steel sabres out in front as their ancestors would have done fighting Napoleon's cavalry on the battlefield of Borodino. As one, we charged, thundering towards the poachers. On seeing the Cossack horsemen and my pack of barking hounds galloping towards them, some of the poachers instantly took flight, trying to flee into the cover of the Taiga Forest, only to find their route to escape cut off by Mishka and Borislav. Other braver poachers stood their ground, desperately pulling machetes out of their belts, unslinging rifles too late. The hounds and my Cossack family fell upon them.

All over the plateau, fighting broke out: horses rearing, kicking and swerving, dogs barking, jumping up on the poachers to protect their masters. A Mongol with molten eyes and bared teeth ran forward with his machete raised at Valentin. I leapt up, biting into his arm. The poacher howled and dropped his machete, allowing me to grab the handle between my teeth and rush away.

The Mongol ripped his rifle free and pointed it at me. With his finger on the trigger, I charged at him, jumping up and sinking my teeth into his hand. Shrieking with pain, he dropped the rifle and lost his balance, tumbling onto his back. The rifle hit a rock and made a loud bang. In fury, I leapt upon him. As the Mongol pummelled me with his flying fists, I bit into the arm of his coat; then, amid my personal battle, Valentin shouted:

'Vinnie, hold. Hold!'

I let go and stepped back. Valentin stood over the poacher, pointing his sabre at the Mongol's throat. The rest of the poachers were being rounded up by the victors. Igor passed the kneeling poachers, eyes filled with sorrow. He shook his big head, then led me towards Mishka, who was leaning over a fallen Vizsla. Running up, my heart broke; it was my dear brother Istvan who lay prone in the snow! Mishka desperately tried to stem the flow of blood from a bullet wound, while my brother's head lay in Borislav's lap. Tears ran down the hard Cossack's ruddy cheeks. The Mongol's bullet had done its deadly work. I stood over Istvan, pawing at his shoulder, imploring him to fight. Istvan's breathing was shallow, and he whispered in my ear: 'No better brother - no better friend.' With that, the light went out of his bright amber eyes.

It was only then we heard a huge roar coming from the other side of a copse of silver birch.

Rushing over, we saw a magnificent tiger lying on the ground, its paw caught in a rusty iron trap. A silver birch branch had lodged itself between the teeth and had stopped the trap from closing fully. The tiger's free front leg thrashed about, its razor-sharp, curved claws slicing into anything that dared to come too close. Valentin and his men ran over and surrounded the stricken beast, trying to decide what to do. The men argued passionately, eventually agreeing that trying to free the tiger's paw from the trap would endanger all of them and that the most humane thing to do would be to put the poor beast out of its misery. With this realisation, my brave Cossack family - all strong men - cried tears of frustration and rage that they hadn't been able to track down the poachers sooner.

Overwhelmed with grief for the stricken Tiger and the loss of my brother, I began to turn away. Suddenly, I felt a presence: Istvan's spirit flowed through me. With his voice in my head, his eyes became mine, and I knew what I must do. I turned to Igor. *Please trust me, old friend.*

Igor gave me a puzzled look but nodded. Unseen, I pushed through the men's legs, crouched down, and crawled towards the tiger. On seeing me, the tiger suddenly stopped thrashing about. Instead, he stared at me, his golden eyes full of pain and torment. I could see his free paw rising, claws drawn to strike me down, but he held his killer blow. Through both our minds, a distant memory flashed. He retracted his claws; the tiger opened his eyes wide in recognition of the cheeky hound who had defied him from long ago. At the same time, I realised this was my tiger; his ripped ear matching my own. His golden gaze never left my amber eyes. A bond of trust began to form between us. I crawled closer. Behind me, I heard Valentin's voice, low but urgent: 'Vinnie no! Come back. Vinnie,

VINNIE!' Ignoring my master's plea, I held the tiger's gaze. All the men fell silent, watching me intently. Mishka whispered to Valentin, 'Vinnie - he's hypnotising the tiger!'

Not quite believing their eyes, seeing the tiger begin to relax, appearing to be calm and still, Valentin quietly ordered two ropes to be brought from the poachers' trucks. Valentin and Mishka each took an end of a rope, crawling forward towards the trap on their bellies. They carefully attached the ropes to the traps rusty iron teeth. Scrambling back, they were joined by two other men who took up the ropes. All leaned back, taking the strain. The ropes went taught as the men began to pull the tiger trap open. With a loud click, the spring locked into place and the man fell backwards, frozen in fear.

With its paw now released from the iron prison, the tiger roared in my face. I shut my eyes, feeling his hot breath rush over my nostrils, thinking that I would be joining Istvan. But then I felt the tiger's steady breathing warming my face, as his long white whiskers tickled my nose. I opened my eyes. He was studying me; his golden eyes now steady and calm. Slowly, he lifted his paw out of the trap and put it down on the snow. Men, horses and hounds held their breath as the tiger put a little weight on his injured paw. Taking his first tentative steps, he slowly turned and began to walk away, a little lame at first but getting more certain with every step. When he got to the line of larch trees, he looked back at the scene of frightened horses, tail-wagging hounds, stunned Cossacks, and in the middle, a lone orange Vizsla with a matching ripped ear.

'Three cheers for Vinnie, my brave Tiger hound!' Valentin cried. All the Cossacks cheered and the pack howled in delight.

After the celebrations and praise, the men then sat down to argue about what to do with the poachers. Some wanted Taiga justice: the poachers would be released unarmed into the Taiga Forest, with a seven-day walk to the nearest village. They would have to take their chances with the numerous wolf packs, bears and even the revengeful tiger. Valentin listened to all the arguments, then raised his hand for silence.

'Comrades, I vote we should take them to the police station in Tomsk, and let the authorities deal with them.'

The Cossacks murmured unhappily between themselves, but then Mishka and Borislav raised their hands in support. One by one, the other men concurred. Only Bohdan disagreed, arguing that in wanting to kill the tiger for financial gain, the poachers deserved nothing less than the law of the Taiga. However, looking round the circle of his united friends and comrades, Bohdan begrudgingly agreed.

The poachers were loaded up into the back of one of their own trucks. Borislav, Bohdan and two other Cossacks jumped in the back to act as guards. The other two trucks were driven into the forest as far as they could go, then the keys were tossed away. Branches were used to cover the vehicles, with one window left open for each. In years to come, they would become a haven for insects, chipmunks and raccoon dogs, serving as a safe home to bring up their young.

In the sole remaining truck with the poachers at the back, Valentin gunned the engine into life and the exhaust backfired noisily, making the horses jump. Before he had a chance to close the truck door, I jumped into his lap. 'You, Vinnie, my faithful hound, will be my good luck charm in the big city.'

For four days and nights, Valentin drove through a Siberian snowstorm. It was a whiteout of blizzards, skidding ice and snow drifts. Only on the fifth day, through a thin haze of specked snow, did we arrive at the old city of Tomsk.

Valentin pulled up the truck in front of Tomsk police headquarters - a forbidding grey, concrete building. An armed policeman opened the glass door at the top of the stairs, eyeing Valentin warily and ordering for the truck's noisy engine to be turned off.

'Why are you here in Tomsk?' he asked Valentin brusquely.

'We just caught a band of tiger poachers and brought them in the back of the truck,' Valentin pointed.

The policeman fingered his moustache and nodded.

'Stay here.'

Valentin watched him march back up the stairs and back into the station. It seemed less than five minutes when the doors to the station were thrown wide open, as around thirty armed officers surrounded the truck, followed by a smart-looking man in his 50s, wearing a heavy black overcoat. Peering in through the truck window, the officer smiled at me, giving me his hand to sniff, which smelt of apples.

'Are you armed, Cossack?' he asked Valentin.

'Only for mine and my men's protection, Sir.'

Valentin drew out his sabre, then his pistol, followed by a knife, before finally handing over his father's rifle. The senior policeman raised his eyebrows, asking Valentin sarcastically if that was all. Valentin nodded.

'That's a handsome dog you have there, Cossack.'

Of course, Valentin enthusiastically told him all about our breed. As he did so, Valentin relaxed, encouraging me to say hello to the officer, who proceeded to give me a lovely long stroke.

'Cossack, I very much like your dog, but I am not so sure of you.'

He turned to one of his junior officers. 'Bring a collar and lead for this lovely hound.' Turning to another officer, he then said quietly: 'Arrest everyone.'

Valentin gasped. 'But what have we done, Sir? We were just bringing these poachers...'

His words faded as two policemen grabbed him and placed cuffs on his wrists, pulling him to the ground.

I barked, totally confused what was happening, straining to leap out the truck. But, before I knew it, the senior policeman had slipped a collar around my neck, attached to a lead. I watched helplessly as all my Cossack friends and the evil poachers were unceremoniously frog-marched up the steps into the police station.

The senior officer knelt and whispered in my ear. 'We'll let those hot heads cool their heels for an hour or so, then I'll find out the truth. Let's go in and find you something to eat - you must be hungry.'

I followed him to his comfortable office, where he ordered a junior officer to go to the canteen and bring back a plate of sausages. I gobbled them up (all very tasty). After eating, in the fashion of all Vizslas, I jumped up onto his lap, curling up to doze off. Speaking into his telephone, he ordered Valentin and the Mongol to be brought into his office. I'd never seen poor Valentin looking so terrified.

'My name is Colonel Alexei Yoshenko. I know nothing of the worlds you two come from but, be assured, one of you will find out all about mine.'

The Colonel first turned to Valentin. 'You, Cossack. Explain yourself.'

Valentin described how he and his men had captured the evil tiger poachers, pointing to the Mongol and saying that he had tried to kill Valentin first with a machete, then with a rifle. Both times his life had been saved by me. Going on, he spoke of how I had hypnotised the trapped tiger, allowing him and his men to open the trap and freeing the tiger's paw. Every time Valentin mentioned the word tiger, I looked up to get a stroke from the Colonel. To Valentin's dismay, some of the police officers in the room began to laugh and snigger at Valentin's story.

The Colonel called for silence, shouting at his men to stop giggling like schoolgirls. He then turned to the Mongol, asking to hear his version of events.

In broken Russian, the man who tried to kill the tiger, me and Valentin then presented himself and his men as innocent gold traders travelling towards Kazan, minding their own business, when from out of the forest came these wicked Cossack horsemen who set their vicious dogs upon them. The Colonel pointed at me. 'A dog like this one?'

'Yes! Just like that one.'

'You wouldn't say you provoked the attack at all?'

'Oh no, sir.'

The Mongol held up his sore hand, then rolled down his sleeve to show my livid red bite marks to the Colonel.

'This Cossack scum set his dog on me, then he robbed me and my fellow travellers of all our money and gold, then brought us to Tomsk police station to try and frame us.'

The Colonel thanked the Mongol politely and turned back to Valentin. 'Cossack, do you honestly expect me to believe your story? It sounds like a fairy tale. I believe it is you who is lying, and it is the Mongol who is telling the truth! I believe you stumbled upon these innocent travellers in what you mistakenly believe is your territory, viciously set upon them and robbing them of their belongings, before finally kidnapping them. That's the truth, isn't it, Cossack?'

Valentin shook his head, seeming about to speak, but then stopping with his mouth open. The Mongol grinned, revealing a mouthful of gold teeth.

'Cossack, you and your men will stand trial for robbery and kidnap!'

Valentin was about to protest but, realising it would be to no avail, hung his head. Then the Colonel said sweetly to the Mongol that he and his men would be free to go. 'Just one last question though. The Cossack claims you attacked him and his dog with a machete.

'Oh no, sir, it was this Cossack scum! He tried to kill me with his vicious sword.'

The Colonel nodded, looking at Valentin. 'Yes, of course, Cossack scum.'

He turned to his sergeant, talking in very fast high Russian, to find a machete. While the sergeant searched, the Colonel made small talk with the Mongol about the high price of gold and seeing a dentist.

The sergeant came back in proudly holding aloft a machete. The Colonel ordered him to wave it around heroically. I looked up, disinterested. The Colonel then asked Valentin to take the machete and swing it round 'like your Cossack Sabre.' I watched my master cut the air half-heartedly.

The Colonel smiled to the Mongol. 'Please take the machete off the Cossack.'

Arrogantly the Mongol grabbed the blade out of Valentin's hand and raised it above his head. Immediately I leapt up onto the Colonel's desk, barking ferociously, baring my white teeth. The terrified Mongol fell backwards off his chair, letting go of the blade. As soon as the sergeant had picked it up, I curled back up on the Colonel's lap. I barely heard him order the Mongol's arrest, and I really didn't take much notice of him unsuccessfully fighting off the sergeant and two other officers - the click of the handcuffs closing around his wrists barely registered. His screams of 'trickster policemen' and 'filthy Cossack scum' went in one ear and came out of the other. Only the sound of the office door being slammed shut made me look up.

Valentin shook his head.

'You're an idiot, Cossack, but a free idiot. However, first, you will bring back the tiger trap and the poacher's weapons.'

The Colonel then ordered his sergeant to hand Valentin back his sabre.

Looking at the sabre's long blade, the sergeant asked Valentin about the names of the great battles etched into the highly polished steel. Valentin described the sabre's long history from the Battle of Poltava in 1709 against the Swedes to the battle of Paris in 1814, which was Emperor Napoleon's final battle against Czar Alexander's Cossack cavalry soldiers, resulting in his defeat and exile to the island of Elba.

Valentin slid the sword back into its sheath. He then stood up proudly, his honour restored.

'Now,' he said, looking at the Colonel, 'may I have my dog back?'

The Colonel was silent for a few seconds, looking down at me. 'Your men will stay here under house arrest, and Vinnie will stay here being looked after by me personally. I think you will come back for Vinnie before your men.'

Poor Valentin didn't know what to say.

The Colonel continued. 'Smile Cossack, you're a free man!'

Valentin nodded, trying to smile. He asked if he could say goodbye to me. The Colonel nodded. Valentin knelt down and gave me a big stroke. As I licked his face, he told me to be a good boy.

After the sergeant led Valentin out, Colonel Alexei leaned down and whispered in my ear: 'Your Cossack master has the cheek to tell you to be a good boy - now that really takes the dog biscuit!'

That evening, Colonel Alexei walked me through the snow to his pretty green clapboard house in the woods. Smoke curled up from the chimney, rising into the frosty air, and I could smell something tasty cooking - Shashlik kebab's perhaps?

My sharp ears picked up a piano playing alongside a girl's voice singing an old Russian folksong. The music and singing abruptly stopped, as a curtain was pulled back, revealing a little face at the window.

Moments later, the front door opened. There stood a pretty girl with locks of blond hair that fell almost to her waist.

'Papa, what have you brought me!'

CZAR ALEXANDER

She ran towards me, enveloping her arms around my neck, whilst I nuzzled her cheek.

'Katya, this is Vinnie. He is a Hungarian Vizsla, come to stay with us for a few days.'

Katya stroked my ears.

'Papa, his ears are so soft!'

'Go and tell your mother we have a guest.'

Katya rushed into the house, shouting as she went. 'Mama, mama, look what Papa has brought me! His name is Vinnie - he's a hungry sizzler.'

Mama appeared at the door and looked at me as if I was a tiger about to eat her. 'It will only be for a few days, Mamushka,' Alexei pleaded. Mama shook her head, then wagged her finger at Alexei.

'No begging at the table.'

Alexei lent down and whispered in my ear. 'She means you, my friend!'

Inside Alexei's home, a roaring fire burnt in the hearth. The delicious smell was stew and dumplings, making me dribble. On the sofa lounged Alexei's two teenage sons, laughing at their put-upon father.

'In trouble for bringing home strays again, Dad?'

Alexei raised his eyebrows and poked his chest. 'And me, the chief of police.' He sat down in his favourite armchair and Katya came to sit on his lap. 'This dog is called Vinnie, and his master is Valentin. He's a giant Cossack who eats little girls.' He tickled his daughter, making her wriggle and giggle.

I was allowed to sleep at the end of Katya's bed, despite Mama's initial protests. Every day, when she had her meals, she would always squirrel away tasty titbits from her plate for me to enjoy under the table. We spent many happy hours playing with each other. I'd never chased a ball before, but she'd throw it high into the air, and I'd leap up to catch it, dropping it at her feet to be praised. Before long, even Mama and Alexei's two teenage sons came to play with me, and I started to feel like I was part of a new family pack. In the late afternoons, I'd sit looking out of the window, watching and waiting for Katya to return from school. In those quiet moments when I was alone in the house my thoughts turned to Valentin. I knew he'd be battling through blizzards of snow to get back to me.

On the sixth day of my stay, Alexei took me into the police station. I was dozing on his lap as he leant over me, working on the reams of paperwork piled up on his desk, when I heard a truck pulling into the yard. It backfired. Sitting up, I was suddenly alert. 'So, Vinnie, your master has returned. Go ahead, go to him.' I jumped down; Alexei opened his office door.

I rushed down the corridor, nearly knocking over two officers, then - to my absolute joy - saw Valentin coming through the main doors. Seeing me, he crouched down, yet I still managed to knock him over; licking, biting and yelping like a puppy. Alexei watched on, smiling benevolently. He held out his hand, which Valentin respectfully shook. 'Cossack, it's good to see you again. Your men have been helping at the timber yard, in the evening enjoying the Tomsk nightlife. Like Vinnie, they will be very pleased to see you, but before you take them back to the Taiga, I'd like you to meet the person who has been looking after Vinnie for you. So please, come to my home for dinner.' Valentin took his hat off, thanked Alexei, and said he would be honoured.

I lay on Alexei's lap on the short journey back to his home, where Katya and her brothers waited on the doorstep. Valentin guided the truck to a gentle stop and climbed out onto the snow, boots crunching with every stride. Katya watched Valentin briefly, before squealing and hiding behind her brother's legs. I pretended to hide with her while Valentin took the boys' outstretched hands and shook them. Crouching down, Valentin laughed at Katya's little voice begging him not to eat her.

'Your father told me that you took great care of Vinnie, for that I am truly grateful,' Valentin smiled. 'I should like to give you something.'

From under his shirt, he brought out a silver medallion on a fine chain and placed it around Katya's neck. Katya held up the silver disc as if it were an Olympic medal.

'Who is this, Mr Cossack?' she asked, tracing the figure carved into the medallion.

'It's Saint Nicholas, patron saint of all Cossacks, so that in turn makes you a Cossack too!'

Katya smiled.

'Thank you, Sir.'

'My name's Valentin.'

'Thank you, Valentin. I have something for you too.' Katya ran into the house and returned with a framed drawing of me with my tiger. Valentin's eyes twinkled as he studied the drawing.

'You keep it child, to remember Vinnie by.'

'No, Mr Cossack, I mean Valentin, I don't need to remember Vinnie with a picture - I'll never ever forget him.' Valentin nodded, took the little frame, and placed it deep in the pocket of his coat. Alexei gave Valentin a brotherly slap on the back.

'Please come inside and meet Galina, my wife. Come, sit at our table and share our food.'

At Katya's side, I led everyone into the house.

With a sense of relief, horses, humans and hounds wearily returned to our home valley. At the camp gates, my pups stood quietly with Valentin's son. Heads bowed and noses twitching, they whined softly as I trotted towards them, scanning the group again and again, searching for the missing piece.

SAINT NICHOLAS

Catherine!

I broke into a gallop and joined my family. We came together as one, overwhelmed with grief. My sons, Peter and Ivan, stayed strong for me; while Anastasia, so like her mother, licked my trembling chin. Catherine was laid to rest in a clearing overlooking the bend in the silver river. I would never forget the first time I really saw her, glowing in the firelight after my battle with Igor, sitting in my prime spot with her head in the air, growling defiantly. The dying embers of the fire shimmered on her copper coat. From that moment, my heart was hers; now with Catherine and Istvan's passing, my heart was broken."

"Vinnie, I am truly sorry. I can't imagine how hard that must have been for you."

"Tovarisch, it is the way of things. Life was often tough in the Taiga, and sometimes we hounds were at the mercy of snow falls and falling branches. Catherine was unlucky, but at least her years were spent well, and she had become a mother. She passed into the next realm in the arms of Valentin's wife, Vera, knowing she was loved by all who knew her."

We sat in silence for a while, watching the dancing embers play.

"So, friend, shall I continue?" I asked.

"Please, Vinnie, I should like to hear your whole story."

"Well, Tovarisch, the following months were sad. Throughout the harsh midwinter, I lost myself in training two litters of the previous year's puppies - teaching them how to stalk silently, when to wait, and when to run. As the snow steadily melted, and our warm coats were taken off, the pups grew in confidence. With the arrival of May, and its springtime sun, they trotted around the camp with their heads high; just like me when I was their age, they thought they knew it all.

Early one morning, Igor pounced on me, barking frantically.

'Comrade, the pups have escaped!'

At a canter, Igor led me to a hole under the stockade fence. Without hesitation, we squeezed through the gap and were greeted with a waft of the pups' scent. With our noses to the ground, we galloped around the still-frozen lake and into the dense Taiga. There, we found musk deer tracks and the unmistakable scent of a chase – paw prints and disturbed earth. We traced the scent, trotting down into valleys, jumping streams and galloping up steep hills until, eventually, their scent grew even stronger. I sniffed the air; the pups were close by.

Igor and I scrambled up to the top of a boulder-strewn hill and puffed a sigh of relief. In the shade of larch pines, sixteen frightened and thirsty puppies panted hard. They surrounded me first, yipping and nipping their thanks, but they couldn't escape Igor's wrath for long. He rose to his full height, eyes bright with furious fire. The pups cowered before him. In our camp, Igor commanded obedience and total loyalty, and commanded no less in the wilderness. He stepped forward to discipline the pups immediately but stopped once he noticed my risen hackles.

The scent that rolled over the clearing was laced with menace. In the far side of the clearing, shadows moved in the long grass.

'We need to go now!' I barked.

From behind a copse of silver birch, a huge grey wolf appeared from the far valley, pushing through the long grass and scrub trees; its yellow eyes bored into us. The leading wolf was joined by another, then another. Soon, the whole pack stood and waited, eyeing us hungrily. When fully grown, one-on-one, we Vizslas were a match for a wolf with our speed, agility and stamina against their power and strength. But, knowing they outnumbered us and sensing our weakness, the wolf pack began to advance slowly, the smell of the puppies' fear luring them in.

Igor and I rushed to round up the pups. With me out in front and Igor in the rear, I charged into the valley, without looking back at the wolves that followed close behind. At the bottom, I ran over a fallen larch tree that spanned a deep gorge and waited for the pups to cross. They hesitated, despite Igor's barking encouragement, and slowly crept along the fallen tree. Across the gorge, Igor ordered me to lead them through Khagan's Pass.

'No Igor!' I barked. 'Igor, we can outrun them. The wolves will tire!'

'No, Vinnie, there's no time.' Igor howled. 'Get them to Khagan's Pass now. Now, comrade!'

With tears in my eyes, I looked at my old friend. He stared down, growling at the rapidly approaching wolves, before glancing back briefly.

'Go Vinnie, go!'

I got behind the pups, ordering them to gallop as fast as they could, not letting them slow for a single moment. As the path forked, I barked at them to turn left, and the pups obeyed my every command. The valley began to narrow on both sides; steep cliffs hemmed us in. Onwards we galloped. The path narrowed again until, in single file, we ran headlong through Khagan's Pass. Igor barked in the distance.

'Get the pups clear! Go, comrade, go!'

My heart ached as I nipped at the pups' heels. On and on, we galloped through the narrow pass. I knew that at the narrowest point of Khagan's Pass, my best friend, Igor the Bold, would turn to face the wolves and hold the line. Like a rock, he would stand and fight tooth and claw, not letting any wolf pass until he fell, overwhelmed by the ravenous pack. Igor's sacrifice gave me new determination. I galloped forward. Not since I had been in my prime had I run so fast. The path opened up, now just two valleys from home, and my lungs burned with the effort. Down we went through the silver birch wood, jumping the stream where we would usually stop for a cool drink, while Igor's defiant snarls and the wolves' howls of rage echoed endlessly. My pack of pups scrambled up the far side of the hill, reaching the path home, on through to the line of giant larch trees that marked the edge of the forest. The path rose steeply; the pups speed faltered. I barked at them angrily to keep going, that home was only the other side of the hill. The panting pups stopped and looked back, their eye's full of concern.

'Go, just go!' I growled, watching them until they disappeared over the hill. With grim resolve, it was my turn to face the oncoming wolf pack. From between the trees, the snarling wolves appeared. Suddenly, they halted at the stream.

Behind me, Valentin led a swarm of Cossacks, waving flaming torches and firing their rifles skyward, to my side. The frightened wolves bolted headlong out of the valley. Halfway up the hill, their leader stopped, threw his head back, and howled with frustration. Then, he too turned and retreated back up the hillside. Mishka, Bohdan and Borislav jumped the stream and galloped halfway up the hill, still firing warning shots until they were satisfied the wolves had gone. Valentin led the thirsty puppies to the stream and let them have their fill. Relief flooded me as the Cossacks returned with their horses unscathed. The pups lapped at crystal clear water so eagerly, it only reminded me of the thirst burning in my throat. I waited for them to drink some more before quenching my own thirst. Valentin gave me a pat; he saw the sorrow in my eyes. Mounting up, he ordered his men to bring back Igor the Bold and ordered me to lead the weary pups back towards the camp. I looked back to see the three riders cantering up the hill towards Khagan's Pass. I would never go that way again.

Valentin's soothing words could not bring back Igor. Distraught and all alone, I made my way to a hole under a larch tree, dug out by a bear in search of honey, and stayed there until Mishka came to me with a large bowl of stew. Climbing into the cramped hole, he lay with me, stroking my back as I ate. He told me how Igor had fought valiantly, taking two wolves with him, but there was no consolation in his words - only sorrow.

Almost overnight, the fur on my muzzle turned snow-white. I wandered around our home valleys, growling away at any hound that came near me, until one night, in my dreams, Igor and Istvan came to me. Both of them looked so young! They were warm to the touch as if their spirits were made whole; their eyes glowed like sunlight through amber. They beckoned me to join them, so I left my warm nest under Valentin's bed, and followed them.

To my surprise, I passed effortlessly through the closed solid wooden door of the cabin as if it wasn't there. Outside we nuzzled each other. Igor winked at me.

'No more sadness, my friend. Both myself and your brother did our duty by the pack just as you would have done.'

Istvan nodded.

'Now, comrade, it is our duty to make you smile again. So, just for a short time, you will be part of our world, and in our world, anything is possible. Shall we fly, comrades?' Igor smiled.

'Fly, Igor?'

Igor winked at me again, turned, and galloped out of the camp. With Istvan by my side, we chased after Igor. Faster and faster, we galloped. My body felt weightless, and then we rose, flying into the dark, star-sparkling night. To my complete and utter joy, Catherine and a multitude of other Vizslas joined us. Together, we streaked across the moon, turning it orange. We flew so high that the wide rivers below shrunk to winding silver ribbons. Landing on the far-off peak of Mount Pobeda, we sat in the snow looking out over our Siberian home. Igor told me to stop being so hard on myself, that my guilt was unnecessary, and that what happened was the natural law of the Taiga. The important thing, he urged, was that we saved the puppies. I knew his words were the truth. When I awoke in my bed, the sun was high in the sky, and a wave of peace washed over me.

My time as a leader ended with Igor's passing. My heart wasn't in it; now was the right time to hand over the reins to our sons. The three hounds worked well together out in front, leading the pack for four seasons. Together with Valentin and Mishka, they ranged all over the Taiga. From Yakutsk on the river Lena in the far East of Siberia, all the way to the western city of Salekhard, which lay beneath the purple shadows of the Ural Mountains. I spent more time in the summer camp sleeping in the vegetable garden. Nicolai, Valentin's son, built a sun-warmed bed for me out of straw bales. There, I was joined by the camp's cats. At first, they were wary, testing my temper with curious paws and slow movements. Soon, they became bold, rubbing up against me, purring and kneading my flanks with their little paws tipped with needle-sharp claws. If I did react, they arrogantly gave me the evil eye and, truth be told Tovarisch, I was a little afraid of these dinky, multi-coloured tigers.

Late in the morning of midsummer's day as I was curled up asleep with my feline friends, a party of Cossack riders galloped into the camp to see Valentin. Their headman, who sold horses, proposed to trade some of our young hounds for a fiery colt to bring new blood into the camp's stable. The two men haggled and argued boisterously, before shaking hands and hugging, marking the deal as struck. Although it was a two-day ride away, Valentin decided to take me on the trip to say my goodbyes to the puppies. I hadn't been for a long run that year and my sons teased me - would the old dog be able to keep up with the fast-running pack?

That night, the men had a party. The camp's boys and girls built a huge bonfire; its flames rose so high, they seemed to lick and warm the cold, white moon. I loved listening to old Russian folk music played on the guitar like Balalika and Domran, accompanied by the Bayan organ. First the Cossacks would sing a mournful ballad remembering their ancestors then the Balaliaka player struck up a faster tempo. Then the men would jump up to perform doing their traditional Cossack Hopak squat dance, each leaping higher than the last. Valentin and Mishka spun their wives in great circles until they collapsed on the floor, laughing, with their children clapping and calling for more.

The following day, all the Cossacks had sore heads and bleary eyes. One tried to mount his horse and tumbled off the other side, landing in a grumbling heap while children laughed and danced around him. His horse looked on with wide eyes and a tail flicking with displeasure. It wasn't until the sun was high that the Cossacks were ready to depart. Leaving by the south gate, the riders pushed their horses into a slow, rolling canter. At that pace, we Vizslas and the Cossack's favorite breed of horse, the Don, could easily eat up the miles.

We came to a vast marsh with a secret path running through it, laid down by the cloven hooves of migrating deer that passed through the swamp over the millennia. The track was only wide enough for the horses to walk single file. Up front, the younger hounds jumped from one grass tussock to the next, keeping up with the leaders. On the narrow path, I followed behind the horses, leading joyful pups who kept jumping into the stinking mud, sending up vast clouds of blood-sucking mosquitoes; their bites and high-pitched whining sending horse, human, and hound into a frenzy of stamping, slapping and scratching. Towards the end of the marsh, we pushed into a vast reed bed. Everyone became wary as the tall reeds, which grew higher than the horses' heads, could conceal hidden predators. The leading hounds disturbed a flock of snow-white cranes; they took off, flying lazily into the air, circling to land only after our passing. Clearing the reeds, it was with great relief to see the light-green leaves of the tall silver birch trees which marked the edge of the swamp, once again breathing sweet air into our lungs. The Cossacks pushed their horses into this newfound freedom at a fast canter. Some of my younger pups galloped on excitedly, overtaking the horses. I ran with them, trying to maintain control on the path which twisted into the high hills, leaving the swamp far behind.

From behind us, a cry went up - wolves! Breaking from the cover of the marsh reeds, the wolfpack ran to our right, galloping hard up the valley to cut us off. Some of the younger Cossack riders panicked; the horses, who sensed their fear, took off and stampeded out of the valley. Panic spread. Even the experienced riders desperately fought to maintain control over their rearing steeds. Hurtling up a steep hillside to a ridge on top of the hill, where the path narrowed, a frightened, swerving horse overtook me. As he passed, he kicked out. A heavy hoof collided with my thigh, sending me hurtling down the hillside. Before I had even reached the bottom, my head hit a rock, and I blacked out.

When I awoke, all was black. I looked up at the rising moon - it was hazy red. I realized the throbbing cut on my head had bled into my eyes. Blinking away the blood, I tried to move. A sharp pain in my leg seared, and night fell upon me once again. When I came to, all was silent. In the moonlight, I took in my surroundings. Above me was the high ridge I had tumbled down; on the boulder-strewn plateau where I lay, three tall larch trees grew. A shimmering, grey blanket of mist covered the entire marsh. All my survival instincts kicked in; I knew all the Taiga's hidden dangers. I had to get myself to the cover of the larch trees. I tried to drag myself along by my front paws, yelping through the pain, as I scrabbled at the stony ground. It was all to no avail, Tovarisch. The permafrost below me had chilled my bones.

I lay there frozen, panting, when I sensed a movement above. On the ridgeline, a shaggy, grey head appeared in the moonlight. Two hard, yellow eyes shone out. I stayed very still, but I knew the wolf's sense of smell was equal to mine, and that they would be able to pick up the scent of my warm blood. Sure enough, the wolf threw back his head and howled. More grey heads appeared on the ridge. Slowly, they made their way down the steep hillside, and on my left, the tall grass moved. A wolf's head pushed through. It was the pack leader, magnificent in his silver coat. Eating me would be sweet revenge for his two fallen comrades and payback for his own painful wounds from Igor's terrible bite. It was cold comfort to know that when the moment came, the wolf would make it quick. The cold seeped further through my bones. I swayed in and out of consciousness. A streak of bright light burned across the sky, turning the moon orange. Suddenly, I didn't care about being taken by the wolves. Igor the Bold was here! But as quickly as he came, he turned and streaked away, the pack following him back towards the moon.

'Igor, no!' I cried. 'Please come back!'

As I began to black out, a terrible roaring and howling filled my head, louder and louder until - silence. Shadows passed over me before I was overwhelmed by darkness. Before going under, I felt a presence very close by, steady warm breathing on my face, then a huge weight slowly lay down on me before unconsciousness finally won.

I awoke to the distant sound of Vizslas barking. Gradually, the noise filled my ears. Over the ridge came Ivan and Peter, followed by the rest of the pack, coursing like an orange waterfall. As one, they poured down the hillside, surrounding me, snuffling, nuzzling, standing on my broken leg, causing me to howl in pain. Igor's sons, realising I was injured, kept the excited pack at bay while my sons stayed close by. They shook their heads.

'You stupid old dog, we've been up all night looking for you!'

'No, no,' I raved. 'You rescued me from the wolves. Last night you lay on me and kept me warm!'

'Calm yourself, father. We've only just found you.'

The pack of hounds began to bay loudly as four horsemen appeared on the ridge. My relief was complete: Valentin, Mishka, and Borislav the healer, dismounted and handed their horse's reins to Bohdan. The men carefully made their way down the hill.

On seeing my broken body, Valentin's eyes filled with tears; he lay down next to me, pulling my ears and whispering soothing words. Borislav examined my leg and paw. He asked Mishka to find a branch of silver birch that matched the curve of my thigh and a straight one for my front leg. Once found, Valentin took off his shirt and ripped off both sleeves. Very carefully, Borislav wound the cotton around my thigh. I yelped in pain as the broken bone knitted back together, the birch branch stabilizing the break, and then again as he did the same to my paw. I licked his face in thanks, his words soothing the worst of the pain away.

Carefully, Mishka picked me up and carried me up the hill to where the horses waited. Valentin mounted up with great care. Mishka and Borislav lifted me onto the front of Spartak's saddle into Valentin's lap. With one gentle arm supporting me, his free hand took up the reins. Quietly, he asked Spartak to walk on slowly. Spartak, instinctively knowing he had a precious cargo aboard, picked his way down the hill back towards the marsh. It was the first and last time, Tovarisch, that I rode on top of a horse. Being up high, I enjoyed the view, but not the bumping of the trot and the lurching of the canter.

Back in the summer camp, Borislav used Plaster of Paris to form a cast around my broken thigh and paw. He charged Nicolai, Valentin's son, to look after me, as that September Nicolai would be going to study Veterinary Science in Moscow. I was to be his first patient! I spent the summer lying on my straw bale bed, joined by my purring friends, now with two litters of kittens. I became their surrogate father, which allowed their hungry mothers to hunt. I loved feeling the kittens snuggle under my broad chest, listening to them purr and mew, dreaming of future mousing with their mothers.

After a few months, my cast was removed. I was a little lame at first, but on my walks with Nicolai, my leg and thigh grew stronger. Soon, I was able to run, leap and jump again. I took myself off for long walks, patrolling the outskirts of the camp, but I felt uneasy; something in the back of my mind troubled me. How had I survived that night? I knew both the hounds and the men had come up with some wild, fanciful theories, but none made any sense to me.

One afternoon, I was dozing in my den under the larch tree, when the spirit of Igor joined me. I hadn't seen my friend since that fateful night. After our welcoming nuzzles, he said to me:

'Vinnie, my comrade, I know you are troubled. Share your troubles with me.'

So, I asked him about that night.

'When you came to carry my spirit away, instead of taking me, you left me to the mercy of the wolves. Why?'

'My friend, that is easy. It just wasn't your time to join us.' He smiled. 'But rest assured, you old dog, I will let you know when your time is up!'

He gave me a wink, but seeing I was still anxious, he became serious.

'Go on, comrade, share your thoughts with your old friend.'

'Well, Igor, tell me how I can see you and feel you. You're warm to the touch, so young and full of life!'

He cocked his head to one side.

'Well, maybe I can help you there too, comrade. In life, sometimes you can love someone so much that the spirit world and the world of the living can come together as one. Then, extraordinary things can happen. That is how I know the answer to your final question. Come, comrade. I have something wonderful to show you!'

Together, we crawled out of my den and galloped off towards the lake. Once again, I felt weightless. Side by side, we took off into the sun, over the hills and valleys we flew, leaving the camp far behind. Below me the marsh stretched as far as the eye could see. On the secret path ran a herd of deer off to find new pastures in the south. Halfway across the marsh, the sun began to set unnaturally fast, dropping out of the sky like a stone. Night descended; the moon rose. Igor flew on. I recognised the ridge on top of the lonely hillside with the three, tall larch pines growing between the boulders. We came to rest on a fallen larch. There, lying on the ground, was a Viszla. My first instinct was to help him - it took me a few seconds to figure out that I was looking at myself. All was still, then my eye caught sight of a movement. High up on the ridge, the wolves appeared and howled. Once again, they started to make their way slowly down the hillside. On my left, the long grass parted; the pack leader pushed through. Stomach churning, I turned to Igor.

'My friend, I shouldn't be here! This doesn't feel right.'

Igor pressed a muzzle into my shoulder.

'Be at peace, comrade. Wait.'

The wolves began to circle me, assessing my threat. Suddenly, they all froze, gazing at the three larches.

To my amazement, out of the shadow of the trees came two magnificent tigers: a huge male and his mate, her belly swollen with cubs. He roared at the wolves, while she hissed and spat. In turn, the wolves bared their teeth, snarling and growling. The leader of the pack, his mind in bitter turmoil, began to back away. The whole pack slowly began to retreat from their easy meal, leaving the Czar and Czarina of the Taiga to their feast. Victorious, the tigers padded over to see what sort of prize they had won. The frustrated wolves watched, howling in bitter anger. The female tiger roared, whipping at them with her razor-sharp claws, causing the wolves to shrink back further one by one, disappearing down the steep path back towards the marsh.

The male tiger triumphantly stood over me. After seeing off the last of the wolves, his mate joined him. She sniffed at me, licked her lips, her jaws slathered at the thought of the coming meal. Igor whispered in my ear.

'Look at the male - like yours, his ear is ripped. Comrade, he's your tiger!'

I could hardly breathe - it really was him! My tiger studied my broken body. His golden eyes opened wide, something in his memory stirred: pain and torture; the wicked two-legged creatures; the orange dog with his calm, amber eyes; finally, release and freedom. He put a heavy paw gently on my chest, testing for life. Feeling my heart still beating, he circled me, head low. I could see he was torn between his wild nature and compassion for me, each sentiment fighting for dominance. His mate followed him around. Opening her jaws, she went to lunge in for the kill. Incredibly, my tiger turned and roared at her, warning her off. The roar became a conciliatory, low growl as if to say he'd hunt for her later. She backed off, spitting fury, her eyes like daggers. He ignored her venom and, very slowly, lay across me, sending his warmth coursing through my body. His mate circled, her temper easing, until finally, she lay next to him, having no understanding of why her wild Czar should save and not take a life. Sniffing me, drooling, she gave her mate a devoted nuzzle. She knew that they would soon eat.

In the east, the sun rose red, and the distinctive barks of Ivan and Peter echoed over the horizon. The tiger's ears pricked up. Slowly, my tiger lifted himself off my prone, broken body. The Czar of the Taiga, followed by his Czarina, disappeared back into the trees to hide, waiting just long enough to see my sons appear over the ridge.

My magical vision began to fade. I awoke back in my den, my mind calm, all troubled thoughts vanished. I whispered words of thanks to my friend and comrade Igor the Bold for giving me the gift of a memory that I would always treasure. I knew that in some far-off part of the Taiga, deep inside his warm mountainside cave, my torn-eared Czar would be lying down surrounded by his cubs. Like my kittens, the cubs would be jumping on his head, chewing his ears and chasing his flicking tail. He'd feign irritation, but his big heart would be bursting with pride and love, while his beloved Czarina would be looking proudly on."

Vinnie stopped talking. He looked deep into the heart of the fire, eyes glowing red, reflecting the orange and black of the burning embers. He turned to me and smiled.

"I'm afraid, Tovarisch, that the stories of my tiger end there. I would never see my Czar of the Taiga again. I see him only in my dreams, and now I have shared my story with you, so will too. I know my tiger, camouflaged behind the larch and silver birch, will have seen Valentin and Mishka pass by, galloping behind the horses and the burnished orange of the Vizsla pack; and I know that he will feel safe. Are you tired, my friend? Your eyes look heavy."

"No, no, please, Vinnie, continue. I simply closed my eyes dreaming of your tiger and your frozen magical home."

"Just so, Tovarisch, just so.

Well, my dear Czar, I shall continue. My days as a useful member of the pack were now over. Nicolai took me for a run every day, and together we developed a special bond as only humans and hounds can have. On sunny days, Nicolai would saddle up one of the horses, riding down to the lake for a swim while his horse lazily grazed on the long rye grass. We would swim in the crystal-

LONDON

BRUSSELS

COLOGNE CATHEDRAL

BATTLE OF WATERLOO
1815

SEELOW 1945 HEIGHTS

WARSAW

MINS

PINSK

BERLIN

KONIN

MOLENSK

BORODINO 1812

MOSCOW

YEKATERINBURG

OMSK

NOVOSIBIRSK

TOMSK

LAKE BAIKAL

clear water; I love to watch the shoals of tiny, silver fish darting around my thrashing legs in the shallows. Sitting stock still on the bank, stealthy Nicolai tickled tiger trout, which, when caught, he would barbecue on the fire for our lunch. We'd lie in the long grass, looking up at the passing cloud formations, trying to see the shapes of different animals.

As the long, hot summer passed slowly into September, Nicolai asked his father whether there was any chance he could take me to Moscow. Initially, Valentin said no. It was his wife who suggested I might live with Valentin's brother, who had an apartment in Moscow, where Nicolai could visit every weekend.

A week later, early in the morning, Valentin and Nicolai packed the horses' saddlebags. The pack of hounds roamed around the horses expectantly, thinking they were going on an expedition. My two boys came running into the cabin, barking loudly, much to Vera's annoyance.

'Father, come now,' they urged.

Up I jumped and bounded out, sending Vera and my sons spinning. When Valentin saw me galloping towards him, leaving my sons to eat my dust, he smiled.

'Come, Vinnie, we're going camping.'

On our second morning camping out, after the tent had been folded away, Nicolai built a fire to cook breakfast. While flames danced in a light breeze, Nicolai glanced at our pile of firewood, now only a handful of twigs, and then up at his father. Thick eyebrows leapt high on Valentin's forehead, gaze unmoving from Nicolai's boyish grin.

'It's your turn,' Nicolai urged.

Valentin sighed and tramped away from our camp, hunting around for fallen silver birch branches - the very best wood to light a fire. In the middle of the meadow, where Valentin had pitched the tent, stood a copse of silver birch trees surrounding four or five towering larch pines. I could smell something sweet in the air as we approached the silver birch. Valentin caught the scent too and looked at me with wide eyes.

'Vinnie, wild honey!'

Together we made our way through the young, silver birch towards one enormous larch tree surrounded by bushes.

Suddenly, my hackles rose. I pulled at Valentin's sleeve, trying to warn him, but he ignored me, intent on putting some sweet, wild honey on his morning porridge. Bees buzzed overhead. Carefully, he pushed aside a bush, only to be confronted by a snarling bear, a halo of enraged bees swarming around its head. The bear rose onto its hind legs, its front paws lashing out at the furious, stinging bees. In alarm, Valentin stumbled backwards. I pushed in front of him, growling and barking, leaping at the bear, matching its ferocious snarl with one of my own. The bear, taken by surprise at my sudden appearance, turned and fled, ambling away across the meadow, taking the swarm of maddened bees with him.

The bear's claws had torn open a deep hole in the giant larch. From the bees' nest within, Valentin scooped out some of the sweet honey into the cup of his drinking flask for himself and Nicolai. Reaching in, he broke off a piece of honeycomb for me. Oh, it was so sweet, Tovarisch, so moreish! I sat down and begged for more. Wild bees and honey - they make just one of nature's wonders. Valentin broke me off a second piece and got down on his knees to feed it to me; then he gave me a hug thanking me for saving his life yet again.

It was, of course, a favour returned, as he and Spartak had bravely saved me when I had first encountered my tiger. But you know, Tovarisch, I think my loud bark would have scared off the tiger as well!

Later that afternoon, we got to the little village with the telegraph station and, sure enough, there waiting behind the counter was Uncle Yakov's reply. Nicolai tore it open and began to read, his eyes scanning the page. Valentin and I looked at him expectantly. Nicolai smiled, handed the telegram to his father, then dropped to his knees, hugging me. 'Vinnie, you're going to see the big city's lights!'

The following week came the day the Cossack riders and most of the hounds would be coming to see us off. We would be running through the Taiga Forest to distant Novosibirsk, the nearest city with a Trans-Siberian railway station. Our journey would be long: we'd all be enjoying six nights in the Taiga under the bright stars. At the camp gates, all the boys and girls, surrounded by the young hounds and pups, waited to say a last goodbye to *Vinnie the Tiger Hound*. The pups jumped up on me, smothering me and giving little bites and nips until Borislav pulled them off. He gave me a big stroke and told me to stay away from the Moscow strays. Finally, he gave my mended thigh a last pat before the camp gates were thrown open. The pack bayed at me to join them, so I trotted to the front to lead the pack into the Taiga for the very last time.

Our final night's camping was in a clearing near the main road into Novosibirsk. On the far side of the clearing ran the river Ob, whilst reflected in its slow-flowing waters were the city lights glowing like multi-coloured electric fires.

The Cossacks would have a final party. Families from the local village were invited to eat and drink. Many were fascinated but also a little frightened of the Cossacks. The people arrived with their shy children to sit around the fire, drink wild honey Medovukha, eat Ukha (a delicious fish soup), listen to traditional music, and watch the Cossacks dance. The children enjoyed meeting us hounds, stroking the horses while the men were invited to try the Hopak dance, making fools of themselves in front of their wives and girlfriends. Everybody laughed and clapped, and when walking home, they all agreed that the Cossacks weren't all that scary.

The next morning, after a breakfast of honey pancakes and strong coffee, the fire was doused down. The men staggered around like bears with sore heads clearing up to leave no trace of their passing. Putting on their best coats, the Cossacks mounted up. This time, the younger hounds and my grand-pups would stay in the clearing to be looked after by their mother Anastasia, father Oleg and Uncle Pavel. Kandybar, the camp cook, would watch over them all. I went to say goodbye to him. When I was a young hound, I drove him to distraction, stealing food whenever his back was turned, but now we were old friends. He gave me a sausage then pretended to kick me, and I pretended to bite his leg. I'd miss his delicious camp stews. I wondered what food I would be eating in faraway Moscow.

My grand-pups surrounded me. I let them knock me over, pinning grand-hound Vinnie down. I loved the feeling of their little pin-sharp teeth nipping at my throat. I'd throw them off only to be attacked again. When I was allowed up, Igor's sons bowed their heads to me, respecting their former master. They led the pups away, leaving me to say goodbye to my daughter. Everything had already been said, so we closed our eyes, our necks entwined, until Valentin told me gently to come. I went to the front to proudly lead my pack into the city of Novosibirsk.

Crossing over the wide River Ob on the Bugrinsky bridge, some car drivers were respectful of the horses and gave them a wide berth. Others, angry that their modern life had been held up for thirty seconds, blew their horns. Sitting in their cars driving away from the frightened horses, they were big brave self-righteous heroes, but truth be told, they were far too cowardly to stand up to a Cossack man to man.

In the city centre, people stopped and stared open-mouthed, watching our happy parade go by. Children jumped and clapped; young women left cafes leaving their coffee to go cold, while others came out of hair and beauty salons, their hair unfinished and nails half-painted, just for a while leaving their mobile phone lives to flirt with these proud, colourful men from a by-gone age.

The Cossacks dismounted and took over the car park at Novosibirsk railway station, watched by a car full of sullen-looking police officers faceless behind dark sunglasses. The men, including Valentin, became subdued - for a Cossack parting is difficult – but, Tovarisch, do not think I was unhappy! Yes, I was leaving my family, but we hounds are optimistic; we can leave the worries of men and the world behind. A new chapter in my long life was about to open, and I wanted to dive in with all four paws.

I had a quiet moment with my sons. As joint leaders of the pack, feeling responsible, they tried to give advice to their old dad. But instead of listening, I ignored their wise words and became a pup again, jumping up on Ivan - bundle game! He threw me off and I leapt on Peter before both boys gave in to the moment; we rolled around playing like when they were pups. The other hounds all joined in, as a ball of joyful Vizsla orange cartwheeled around the car park. My Cossack family looked on and clapped, with even the faceless policemen smiling at our antics, reflected in their mirrored sunglasses. Saying goodbye to my human friends was different from my Vizsla family. For humans, leaving any animal can be very moving. Bohdan gave me a big bear hug. I sniffed around his jacket, as he always had a tasty treat for me, and sure enough, he pulled out a piece of deer jerky that I sat for. I haven't tasted jerky since coming to England - its rich, smoky taste is just one of the things I have missed. I then went up to Mishka.

Mishka, oh Mishka, always the emotional one. He dropped to his knees, tears welled up in his eyes, and began rolling down his face into his beard. Together we had shared so many memories. I licked his face, which was my way of saying no tears, just joy.

Finally came my master, Valentin. I leapt up onto his shoulders for the last time. He put his arms around me, holding me so tight I could feel his big heart beating. Letting me go, he asked me to sit; from out of his pocket, he took a collar and lead. The collar was made from a very fine deer hide, into which Valentin had tooled my name. On either side, leaping tigers were cut into the leather, inset with tiny pieces of amber for their eyes. I still wear the collar today, Tovarisch, look!

Valentin hugged his son before he handed him my lead. I followed Nicolai towards the station doors. Looking back, the Cossacks were mounting up. My pack of hounds milled around the stamping horses' hooves, all wanting to get back to the forest. I took a last backwards glance. Mishka looked up and waved. I barked; he blew me a kiss. As if by magic, the station door opened. Nicolai led me through, then - with a whoosh - the doors closed behind me, and I said a final goodbye to my Taiga life.

I sat on the marble floor in the concourse of Novosibirsk Station. Looking up at the ceiling, it was like being inside a light green egg. Neither Nicolai nor I had been in such a vast building. The other biggest building I had been in before was a beautifully ornate Russian Orthodox church three days ride away from the summer camp. Every year Valentin would take me to a service dedicated to all animal friends and the wild beasts of the Taiga. Yet, the interior of Novosibirsk station dwarfed the church.

Admiring the station, we were ignored by hundreds of our fellow passengers in their own little worlds, but then I noticed a most striking lady walking towards us across the concourse, her high heels tip-tapping on the marble floor. Ignoring Nicolai, she went down on one knee, held out her arms, and cried: 'Oh my, a Vizsla!' I padded up to her, and she stroked me sensuously; her fingertips were topped with long green, painted talons. Nuzzling her neck, I smelt roses and long summer Parisian days. She whispered sweet nothings in my ear in a language I had no understanding of before she stood up and introduced herself to Nicolai. 'I am the Countess Restikova. Who are you, and what is your handsome Vizsla's name?'

Nicolai blushed, gushing, 'I'm Nicolai, I'm a Cossack, and my hound's name is Vinnie.' She raised a painted eyebrow, looking him up and down. 'You are indeed a Cossack.' She held out her hand, which Nicolai shook awkwardly. She seemed a little taken back. 'Manners, Cossack! You may kiss the hand of a countess when offered.' Nicolai blushed an even deeper shade of red as he kissed a large, cold emerald set into a platinum ring. The countess seemed happy enough and bent down to give me a long languorous stroke. She asked Nicolai if we were travelling to the capital. Nicolai explained that he was going to university in Moscow. 'Then you and Vinnie must join me as my guests for dinner.' She pointed her emerald at an office. 'You buy your ticket there. Cossack. I will send for you and Vinnie at eight.' In a haze of summer flowers, she tip-tapped away, leaving Nicolai open-mouthed.

After buying our third-class ticket, Nicolai stowed his case away. Looking up the platform to his amazement, the locomotive wasn't a stinky diesel, but a magnificent blue steam engine. Nicolai asked the third-class conductor if there was time to see the engine. She smiled at his boyish enthusiasm, telling him he had fifteen minutes. Thanking her, he led me up the platform. When we got to the first-class carriages, we looked up through the window and glimpsed the countess giving the conductor a tongue-lashing. Noticing us, she turned and smiled, waving. Nicolai waved back half-heartedly, not really sure if her wave was for him or me. The countess pointed down at me, mouthing something to the conductor. We didn't need to be able to lip-read to work out that dogs were not allowed in first-class. Nicolai leant down to me. 'Looks like dinner's off, Vinnie.'

We left them to their arguing to go and look at the steam engine, partly obscured by light grey smoke. The engine tender and boiler were dark blue with a gold stripe, with six huge red wheels to power the metal beast along the rails. I could see why Nicolai thought it was magnificent. On the front of the train was painted a Soviet red star. Nicolai patted the engine like he patted me - for, in his mind, this clanking hissing dragon was as much alive as either him or me.

Hearing the shriek of a warning whistle, we ran back to our carriage, where Nicolai was quickly shown to his seat before another whistle sounded. So comfortable was the train that, at first, it didn't feel like we were moving at all; only looking out at the disappearing suburbs of Novosibirsk gave the game away. Nicolai settled down with a textbook on horse anatomy; I went to sleep on his lap.

We must have must fallen asleep at some point in the journey, for I became aware of the rather angry, flustered conductor we had first seen in the first class carriage. He shook Nicolai. 'Young man, your name and that of your dog, please.'

Nicolai stammered our names.

'Thank you. You and your dog are cordially invited to join the Countess Resticova for dinner. Please follow me.'

Nicolai quickly combed his long blond hair and attached my lead. I jumped up and down excitedly, almost pulling Nicolai's arm out of the socket. 'Vinnie, heel. Heel!' He ordered, reluctantly I obeyed. All the passengers turned to look at me and smiled. My twitching nose was filled with the smells of

Schi cabbage soup being warmed up on a camping stove and Rye bread being broken. We followed the conductor up through third class into the sky-blue second-class carriages. From the sleeping berths above, excited children unable to sleep called down to Nicolai, asking for my name and my breed.

We continued further on through the second-class carriages until the conductor opened the door into first-class. We found ourselves transported into a magical world of luxury; even my paws were greeted by deep, springy carpets, softer than the Taiga snow. The seats were covered in plush red velvet, with equally plush-looking travellers sitting atop. The windows and ceiling were ornately carved from the finest teak. Between panels of painted glass, elaborate lights cast a warm glow.

As we entered the spectacular dining car, the first-class passengers stopped eating their delicious meals to stare at me, walking down the aisle with surprise and fascination. Then I saw her - stunning in a dark green dress setting off her fiery red hair. She called my name and I ran to her, pushing past the shocked conductor, nearly bowling him over, pulling my lead out of Nicolai's hand before jumping onto her lap. She purred with delight, although the conductor strode up with a face of thunder. 'Countess. Your guest Mr Nicolai Malantov and his dog, Vinnie.' She smiled thinly, then waved her hand and glanced at Nicolai.

'Would you like anything to drink?'

'Just water, please.'

The countess laughed, before ordering the conductor to bring his finest vodka.

The conductor bowed his head. 'Immediately, my lady.'

She beckoned Nicolai to sit. 'I had to use all my charms to bring you and Vinnie to me tonight,' she whispered, leaning forward.

Her smile brought out the smoky kohl black depths of her eyes. Nicolai seemed lost in them.

The conductor brought a silky rug for me to sit on, while Nicolai and the Countess ate their scrumptious feast. As I dozed, Nicolai told her about all my many adventures. Every time he said the word tiger, like in the police station, I looked up. She stroked my ears, calling me a brave hound. She, in turn, told Nicolai about her life - her mother was Hungarian, her father Russian, and her grandparents lived near Budapest with a long interest in breeding Vizslas. She loved visiting Hungary to see the hounds at play, riding her pony around lake Balaton. As she spoke, she stroked my back and sighed. 'Truly you are magnificent, *Vinnie the Tiger Hound,*' she said, more than once.

The conductor returned and bowed low to the countess. 'Our chef has prepared a dinner for Vinnie; his presence is requested by Chef Anton.'

I wagged my tail, nearly knocking over the countess' glass of champagne. Nicolai smiled, telling me to go. I jumped down, letting the conductor take my lead and walk me to the galley. As he loudly knocked on the door, I heard indistinct angry shouts.

We were suddenly engulfed in hot steam as the door was flung open. A bear of a man stepped out, red ruddy cheeks glowing with sweat. Under his nose grew a twirly moustache, pointed bright red from tasting Borscht soup. On his head he wore his badge of honour - a bright white toque blanche hat. He raised his arms high. 'Vinnie, I am Chef Anton. Welcome! You have come for your dinner, yes? Your first course shall be the finest Steak tartare which I have served to members of at least three royal families and four presidents. You shall enjoy what the ungrateful proletariat that we have onboard the train tonight didn't finish.' He went back into the galley, coming out with a large bowl of meat. Just as he was about to place it down for me to gobble up, a Commis chef hurried out of the galley.

'Chef, wait, Vinnie can't have your Steak tartare!'

'What do you mean? Vinnie can't eat my steak?'

Chef Anton waved his arms in the air, telling us all once again about the royalty and presidents who had eaten his Steak tartare.

The Commis chef put his hand up. 'Chef, please, dogs can't eat raw onion! I'll take it out for him.'

'Ahhh yes, of course. How remiss of me. Thank you, Pasha.'

When the bowl was returned, I wolfed it down. You know, Tovarisch, I'd never tasted the like; the steak just melted in my mouth; the tartar was followed by beef stroganoff, and again I'd never tasted such a succulent creamy dish. Lastly, a bowl of ice-cold spring water washed it all down. Chef Anton picked up the bowls and put his nose in the air. 'Licked clean bowls, that is what I like to see!' He turned towards the corridor and raised his voice. 'Not leaving good food like those rich peasants out there in the carriage.'

The conductor smiled nervously, then took my lead and walked me back to Nicolai and the Countess, who was now sitting next to Nicolai, and who he now called Sophie. I lay looking at them. Nicolai had a silly, dreamy look on his face, although the countess' expression reminded me more of the slavering Czarina of the Taiga, who wanted to eat me up!

With a full tummy, I fell fast asleep. It was gone midnight when Nicolai led me back to our comfortable sleeping berth. Lying on his legs, I curled up to dream, and to my joy I was visited by Igor. We lay together, happily snuggled up, listening to Nicolai breathing

For three nights, we joined Sophie for dinner. The two of them spent the final day before Moscow in her cabin playing backgammon, while I looked out of the window, watching my Siberian home disappear behind the Ural Mountains.

Early in the evening, the express pulled into Moscow's Kazansky Station in a cloud of smoke and steam. Passengers who had been lazing around reading books and magazines or listening to music flew out of their seats, hurriedly pulling down cases. Some of them had travelled from far off Vladivostok - over 5700 miles away. A few would remain lifelong friends, having shared the experience of travelling on the world's greatest railway line. Sophie and Nicolai let the world go past them before they alighted, hand in hand. They walked down the platform, followed by a sweating, red-faced porter dragging along a cart loaded with Sophie's cases and boxes. At the entrance to the station, her cases were loaded into a car. She kissed Nicolai lightly on the lips. 'Lapochka, I see you tomorrow, yes?' Nicolai nodded. She crouched down, hugging me. 'I see you again soon, my tiger hound.' I nuzzled her neck, alive with the smell of Japanese winter jasmine.

Sophie had told Nicolai to experience the Moscow Metro before doing anything else. So, after buying a ticket, we made our way to the Metro station entrance. A pretty lady wearing a blue uniform and red hat frowned at Nicolai. 'Your dog will have to be carried down the escalator.' Escawhater? Nicolai looked confused. She smiled at him. 'A moving staircase, sir, you'll know it when you see it.' In the distance, we watched people walking, then suddenly disappearing, as if they had fallen over a waterfall. Walking on, we came to the beautifully panelled escawhater. Other passengers just stepped on, descending into the depths of the station. How hard could it be? Nicolai picked me and his case up. Gingerly, he stepped onto the moving stairs then immediately lost his balance, pitching forward with his feet *tripping the light fantastic* as if performing an impromptu Hopak Cossack dance. Somehow, he righted himself. Going down, there wasn't much time to admire the surrounding artwork before the stairs just disappeared into the ground. Nicolai jumped, landing on two feet. A man in a suit looked at Nicolai as if he was completely mad, but Nicolai didn't care, he had defeated the escawhater! At the platform, the train had already arrived and I leapt onboard like I was jumping a river gorge.

We were due to meet Uncle Yakov at the entrance of Komsomolskaya Station. Pulling in, the magic doors opened and we jumped down into an underground palace painted the colour of sunflowers. The walls and ceiling were decorated with beautiful oil paintings surrounded by snow-white alabaster plaster, the chandeliers were works of art in gold and cream. If there were such a thing as the Czar of all badgers, then Komsomolskaya station would be his subterranean home.

Along each side of the station ran a spectacular series of arches leading up to the most magnificent and ornate, though terrifying, escawhater. Up, up it went to the surface, never stopping. Once again, Nicolai picked me up. A kindly old gentleman offered to help by carrying Nicolai's suitcase. Nicolai graciously thanked him and tried to follow him onto the moving steps, but because he was carrying me, he couldn't hold on to the rail. Suddenly thrown forward, his feet danced a jig and the gentleman had to grab Nicolai to steady him. At the top Nicolai got his timing right, jumping off the disappearing steps. After putting me down, he bowed, thanking the gentleman, then followed the crowd of people to a noisy Moscow Street.

There, waiting at the corner, was a black car. Its tinted window was wound down and a man who looked a little like Valentin but was much thinner stared out. Uncle Yakov was more reminiscent of old photographs of Rasputin the Mad Monk than his good-looking brother.

Nicolai waved cheerily. 'Uncle Yakov, it's good to see you.'

'You too, nephew, put the dog in the back.' Nicolai opened the door revealing a dirty back seat, covered in fast-food rubbish. Nicolai began to tell his uncle what I liked to eat and how long I needed to walk. Yakov interrupted, 'I know how to look after a dog, nephew. I am late for an appointment. I say goodbye.'

With that, he drove off, speeding into the Moscow traffic. I jumped up onto the parcel shelf, looking back, watching as Nicolai waved. I barked and barked, not taking my eyes off him, until Yakov turned a corner. Being a friendly hound, I went to sit next to Yakov, but he pushed me back roughly. He smelt of sweat - not the sweat of a hard-working Cossack; Yakov smelt of something dead. Dejected, I lay on the backseat, a half-eaten burger lay in the footwell. Something told me I should eat it, so I chewed down the greasy meat. Yakov lit up a filthy cigarette and opened the back window a bit, letting me look outside as we passed a cathedral that resembled a multi coloured wedding cake.

Further on, Yakov drove through the grey Moscow suburbs before turning into an underground car park. He roughly pulled me out. A younger Vinnie may have tried to escape but, truth be told, Tovarisch, I was too scared. He dragged me into a stinking lift, it jerked noisily upwards until the doors opened onto a corridor where a single light flickered. Passing two doors, he took out his mobile phone, which I mistook for a biscuit and jumped to get, only for Yakov to raise his arm to hit me. I shrank away from the coming blow.

He made a brief call. Inside the apartment, I heard locks being unbolted before the door opened. Meekly, I followed Yakov inside, where two men waited in expensive designer suits, one grey and one black. There was a cage by the door and Yakov was instructed to put me inside and lock it. The three men discussed the price to be paid for me, and they began to argue. The man in grey pulled out a bunch of ruble notes and handed them to Yakov, who smiled. Then, without a second glance back at me, he left the room. The man in black kicked the cage, sending me cowering to the back of my prison. The two men laughed, turned off the single light bulb, and slammed the door behind them, leaving me in virtual darkness. As my eyes adjusted, I looked around, taking in my surroundings. At the back of the room was a window with a black curtain pulled across, through a tiny gap poured a bright sunbeam. As the sun moved across the sky, the shard of sunlight progressed slowly across the wall, eventually bathing me and the cage in a macabre spotlight before moving away.

That evening, after the sun had set, the room turned chilly. The two men came back into the room with a hungry-looking woman. While the man in black was pulling me out the cage, they told her that I was her responsibility. He buckled on a collar with spikes lining the inside so that if I pulled they would stab into my neck and gave the lead to the woman, threatening her. 'Don't try anything, you know the consequences! Tomorrow the dog's training will start.'

The woman led me through an interior door into a normal, smart-looking apartment. Other hard, sour-faced men and women lazed around smoking and drinking. I was grateful that they all ignored me. Then I noticed, there sitting in a corner, was the evil Yakov. On seeing me, Yakov spat and made a joke. The woman just led me out, down four flights of stairs, through a pair of glass doors and out onto a bustling Moscow Street.

The woman walked me to a park with a lake. Swans swam between a mass of beautiful teal and Mandarin ducks, but I had no eyes for such beauty. Other dogs being walked saw me but all sensed something was wrong and wouldn't come near me, drawing back as if my mistress walked with a tiger. The woman sat down on a bench overlooking the lake and looked at me. Tears welled up in her hazel eyes. She stroked my head so softly I barely felt her fingers. Looking at me with her sad eyes, she said, 'My name is Tatiana. If I could, I would release you and let you go free, but they would harm my family if I did. I am a prisoner of those vile men too, so please be good for me, and I will do my best for you.' I understood the fear in her eyes more than her words. I nuzzled up to her, feeling her tears fall.

Walking down a fashionable street, we passed cafés; their window displays quite magical with chocolate cakes, cream pastries, and tarts bursting with multi-coloured fruit. Tatiana tied me up outside one of the cafés before going inside. With the little money she had, she bought a ham and cheese croissant. Taking one bite for herself, she fed me the rest, smiling as I ate, and whispered, 'Vinnie, one day I promise we will come back to this café and together we will eat cake.'

The next day, the training started and I discovered I was to be a guard dog. If I heard any sound in the corridor outside, I was to bark. To teach me, the man in black went into the corridor, then made a noise. At first, I didn't react, so the man in grey kicked the cage violently, telling me to bark. The second time I heard the sound, yet again I didn't react, and once more he viciously kicked the cage. I cowered away from his boot. The third time I heard a noise, I barked and barked. The two wicked men tested me throughout the day until they were satisfied, then they let me be. So, this was to be my world! I howled for Igor and Istvan that night until the door was angrily thrown open and an iron bar thrown at the cage, silencing me.

Days and nights passed and through the door I would hear men and women shouting. Sudden, heavy bangs on the wall made me jump, and I could not imagine what was happening on the other side. Only my survival instinct and Tatiana's generosity kept me going.

On the fourth night, I felt a presence. There, standing at the cage door, was Igor and Istvan. I mewed like a puppy, so happy was I to see them. As if the bars of the cage weren't there, they pushed into the prison. My friend and brother shook their heads in dismay as I pleaded with them, 'Please take me with you!'

'Brother, we cannot take you with us, it's not your time, but we can take you away while the evil men sleep and fly you back home. In fact, we can take you anywhere you wish to go.' Igor put his big paw on my shoulder, once again, he said, 'Shall we fly, comrade?'

As if the steel bars had disappeared, I walked out of the cage and through the outside wall to take off, flying high above the apartment block over the wedding cake cathedral and the Kremlin Palace. We became an orange arrow streaking across the sky, leaving Moscow far behind. In the moonlight below, I saw the Trans-Siberian Express on its silver rails making its way to Vladivostok, we flew on coming down in my Taiga home near the vast blue lake where only a month before Nicolai and I had swam. We watched Peter, Ivan, and Igor's boys leading the pack. Galloping behind them through the shallows rode Mishka and Valentin their horses splashing up fountains of water as they waved their sabres shouting, 'Go boys, go.' Watching the pack disappear into the Taiga, my brother and best friend comforted me while I cried for my lost world. I awoke feeling more myself. With my comrades' help and Tatiana's kindness, I believed I could survive my imprisonment.

Over the next four nights, Igor and Istvan came to me, taking me away from my personal Gulag, flying together all over my Taiga homeland: from our summer camp home, onto far away Lake Baikal, over the mysterious island of Sakhalin in the Sea of Okhotsk, up to the frozen wastes of northern Siberia on the edge of the Arctic Ocean. I asked Igor if he was able to find Nicolai. 'It's possible, my friend,' he replied.

The next night, my comrades flew me to a very swish part of Moscow to a restaurant in the sky, all made of glass. The roof curved like Moscow railway station, and we peered through the glass. There at a table sat Sophie and Nicolai smiling, their eyes fixed on each other, their hands entwined. On her ring finger was an emerald and diamond cluster much smaller than the others but far more significant. I was very glad they had found each other, both looking so happily in love. I woke up in the cage smiling.

On the tenth day of my captivity, I heard raised voices, lots of bangs, what sounded like boxes being dragged around, followed by laughter, and champagne glasses being chinked. I heard the evil Yakov shouting, over and over: 'now we'll be rich, rich!' Their celebrations went on for most of the night.

Towards dawn, when all was silent except the sound of drunken snoring, I was sensed a movement. I opened one sleepy eye to see Igor appear out of the wall, just as my sharp ears heard a noise in the corridor. There was a rustle followed by a low voice. I made to bark, but Igor shook his head. I heard his commanding voice in my head, 'Do not bark, comrade!' I heard more whispering, and as my conditioning set-in, my need to bark began to overwhelm me, but Igor firmly held my gaze. Just like I had done with my tiger, Igor's steady eyes calmed me, so I did not bark. Ten seconds later there came an ear-shattering bang as the outside door splintered. Immediately, the inside door opened, the apartment light silhouetting the suited men and Yakov. All three were armed with pistols, the man in grey screaming at Yakov. 'Your useless dog didn't warn us!' As Yakov took aim at me the splintered door flew off its hinges, and a mass of police officers poured into the room.

The three evil men opened fire into the black crowd; the officers fired back. Yakov was hit in the thigh. He screamed, falling back, crawling to hide behind an armchair. One of the officers took a bullet in the chest. The impact of the bullet picked him up, throwing him headlong into my cage. He slumped broken like a rag doll behind my prison. Realising all was lost, the two evil men tried to escape back into the main apartment. The one in black turned, firing into the oncoming policemen, but he was brought down in a hail of automatic machine gun fire. The man in grey, now out of bullets, was hit hard by a truncheon, tackled to the ground and handcuffed. More officers poured into the apartment. Shouts of, 'Clear, clear!' went up. Then, through the smashed door came a very smart-looking officer. I didn't see his face as my attention was drawn to Yakov, whose bony fingers appeared from under the armchair, reaching out for his weapon. Grabbing it, he stood up and aimed at the senior officer. I barked and barked - one of the policemen in black launched himself across the apartment to shield his boss just as Yakov's gun fired. His bullet tore into the policeman's back. Every one of the officers fired their guns in response, sending Yakov to the hell he deserved. The policemen then ripped the apartment apart, looking for other hidden gunmen. Once satisfied, the policeman took off their helmets, their grim faces full of hard resolve.

My attention was held by the policeman who had so heroically taken Yakov's bullet. To my surprise, he slowly pulled himself off his boss and I heard an indistinct voice. 'Sergeant, you need to lose some weight!' Some of the officers began to laugh nervously at the joke. The sergeant gave his boss a hand, pulling him up. The senior officer thanked him for his bravery and shaking his hand he said, 'What I meant to say was, you need to lose some weight, Lieutenant!'

The newly promoted lieutenant lifted the visor of his helmet, beaming a huge smile. 'Why, thank you, sir!'

'Taking a bullet, even with body armour, is a very courageous act!' The other officers surrounded their newly promoted colleague, congratulating him by slapping his back and shaking his hand.

'Lieutenant, I am very grateful for your swift action, but how did you know I was in danger?'

'It was the dog's barking that warned me, sir.'

'Dog, what dog? Where?'

'In the cage, sir, over there.' I heard the approach of footsteps. I was too frightened to look up, but I knew I was being studied.

'Why, it's a Vizsla, they are lovely dogs.'

I heard the cage being unlocked. Finally, I looked up into my Alexei's eyes! We recognised each other immediately. I leapt on him, whimpering and licking his face, covering him with slobber. He kept repeating, 'Vinnie, Vinnie, what have they done to you?' Even some of the tough, grizzled policemen had tears in their eyes. Somehow Alexei got me to sit long enough for the spiked collar to be removed and led me through to the main apartment.

Four other men lay on the floor of the main apartment, their hands cuffed with hard-looking policemen standing over them. Poor Tatiana sat in a chair. Her hands were also cuffed behind her back, her make-up smeared by tears, as police officers shouted at her. I trotted to her and jumped up to sit on her lap, barking and snarling at the policemen to leave her alone. When they backed off, I nuzzled into her neck. Once again, she burst into tears. Alexei watched my actions carefully, then ordered Tatiana's handcuffs to be removed. I felt her relief as she gave me a grateful stroke. Alexei asked her very quietly, 'You know Vinnie? He clearly likes you! I know Vinnie too; he is an extraordinary dog and an excellent judge of character. You tell me what you know, and I will tell you all about Vinnie.'

Tatiana's story came flooding out, her tears making my head wet. Alexei listened, nodding, then told Tatiana all about me. For the first time, I saw Tatiana smile. I knew then that our shared ordeal was finally over. Alexei called over a policewoman and spoke to Tatiana. 'You go with my colleague. She will take care of you.'

'Sir,' Tatiana pleaded, 'can I see Vinnie again before I go back to Georgia? You see, I made him a promise.'

Alexei nodded. 'You have my word that you will see Vinnie again.'"

I rested my head on my friend's broad back. He felt my big tears fall. "Tovarisch, there's no need for you to cry." Vinnie put his big paw over my shoulder. "What happened was a terrible thing, but that experience taught me never to give up; something good may be just around the corner. The way I see it is, if it hadn't happened, I would never have come to England and met you! The experience taught me to never take life for granted; it's a very special gift. I know together we will make some tip-top memories. Yes, Tovarisch?"

"Yes, Vinnie, absolutely tip-top!"

"So Tovarisch, shall I continue?"

"Yes please"

"So that evening, Alexei walked me home to his apartment just off Red Square. He told me that the wedding cake cathedral was called Saint Basil's. Pointing to the other side of the square, he continued. 'That's the Kremlin, Palace of the Red Czars. Where I work is just beyond it.'

We arrived at a smart apartment block. We went up in a lift until the doors opened onto Alexei's front door. He took out his keys, went down on his knees, and cuddled me. 'I haven't told Katya you're here. She will be delighted to see you.' As he turned the key, I heard a sweet voice I recognised. 'Papa's home Mama, I bet he's forgotten the smoked salmon for the blinis.' Alexei slapped his head and gave me a pained expression. As he opened the door fully I saw Katya. 'Hello. Papa, did you...?' On seeing me, Katya's eyes widened in wonder. 'Vinnie, Vinnie! You've brought back Vinnie, Papa!' I ran to her, once again overwhelmed by her love for me and mine for her. From out of the living room waddled a heavily pregnant Mamushka. She smiled at me but waved a finger at Alexei. 'Husband, as usual you have some explaining to do. I take it there is no smoked salmon, just that Cossack's hound again.'

The week I spent with Katya was one of my happiest, but I knew deep down that Moscow would not be my final home. I was sleeping on the end of Katya's bed when Alexei came in with a sad look in his eyes. Katya cuddled up to me. Reading her father's expression, she took his hand. 'It's alright, Papa, I know our apartment is too small. Vinnie is a country dog - he needs to run and be free.' Alexei nodded, not really surprised at his daughter's wisdom.

'Well, lapochka, I thought long and hard about what to do for the best. I will of course try contacting Valentin the Cossack, I know now from the woman Tatiana that he sent Vinnie to Moscow in good faith, but that is all I know. Letting Valentin know what has happened to his beloved dog will be very difficult. If he is away in the northern Taiga, we may not get a response until the Spring. Vinnie needs a good home now, so I have telephoned my friends Ian and Helen who live in England. He is a policeman who looks after retired police dogs. I have arranged to meet him and his wife in Berlin. I will be driving there at the weekend.' Katya looked upset but Alexei took her hand. 'Can you guess who's coming too?'

Katya's face broke out into a smile. 'Thank you, Papa,' she gushed, 'then will you allow me to have a Dachshund like we talked about?'

'Yes, darling, on your next birthday,' he replied, wondering how he would break the news to Mamushka.

The following morning, Alexei called for Katya to join him at the dinner table. I trotted along next to her, not wanting to leave her side. He asked her to sit down and I climbed onto her lap, yawning. Alexei unfolded a large map and pointed to Moscow. 'I thought you'd like to see how far Vinnie has travelled and how far he has to go.' From Moscow, he traced his finger east past the ancient city of Perm, crossing the Ural Mountains to Yekaterinburg, down to Omsk, the city of my birth, and on to Tomsk, where I first met Katya. 'Do you remember your Siberian home?'

'Of course, Papa.'

'What's your favourite memory?'

'In November before winter proper, I liked to watch the icicles growing from the leaky gutter. The snow and ice would melt each day, freezing at night, thawing slightly in the morning. Every day the icicles slowly grew until they were longer than Valentin the Cossack's sabre. When the days turned so cold, they froze to solid silver and when the icicles disappeared, for me, that was the first day of spring.'

'That, lapochka, was what I thought you'd say.'

'And your favourite memory, Papa?'

'That's easy, the day of your birth!'

'Papa, you're silly!'

Alexei smiled, shrugging his shoulders. 'Well, you did ask.'

Alexei traced his finger south from Tomsk. 'Tatiana, the woman we rescued with Vinnie told me she overheard the gang say that Vinnie had boarded the Trans-Siberian Express at Novosibirsk, which is here in southern Siberia. In his long life, Vinnie would have galloped all over the Taiga, probably even quenched his thirst as far off as Lake Baikal.' Alexei pointed out a vast lake in the shape of a croissant, before his finger traced back to Moscow. 'But now, Vinnie's final journey to his new family in England, of course, starts here in the capital. Our first stop will be the battlefield of Borodino, where I can teach you about how Valentin's Cossack ancestors fought valiantly for Czar Alexander against Napoleon's French cavalry. It was a battle which Napoleon won but, in the end, he lost the war and his liberty. Our second stop will be the city of Smolensk, and then we'll drive onto Minsk, the capital of Belarus. Next is Warsaw, Poland's capital, and our final stop is Berlin, the capital of Germany and the ....' he paused, sighed, then continued. 'Where Vinnie will meet his new family. He will then travel through Germany into Holland, down into Belgium, whose capital is Brussels.' Alexei pointed to a little town below Brussels. 'Can you read its name?'

Katya leaned over me. 'It's the town of Waterloo, Papa, the site of Napoleon's final defeat.'

'Absolutely correct. I'm going to ask Ian and Helen, if they have the time, to take Vinnie to the site of the battle. I should like to be able to tell Valentin that Vinnie went there when I see him again. Leaving Belgium, Vinnie will go on to Calais in France and sail on a ferry to England. We will be leaving on Saturday, but tomorrow we are going to meet Tatiana, as I have a promise to keep with her.'

The next morning, a police car waited outside Alexei's apartment. The rear door was held open by Lieutenant Sasha, the man who had saved Alexei's life. Sasha saluted, 'Morning General, morning Miss,' he crouched down, 'morning Vinnie.' I jumped all over him, very happy to see him again. 'Where to, Boss?'

'The David Bowie Café, do you know it?'

'Bolshoy Palashevskiy, best coffee in Moscow, sir.' Sasha talked about music with Katya while Alexei and I looked out of the window, watching Moscow life pass by. Outside the David Bowie Cafe waited Tatiana.

Seeing her, I strained at my lead until Alexei let go. I raced to her, and this time there were no tears, only laughter, followed by Ziggy Stardust sausages, ice cream sundaes, milkshakes, and honey and chocolate croissants.

When Saturday came, as Alexei loaded the cases in his car, Mamushka came to see us off with tears in her eyes. She knelt down, taking out a little bag to reveal a few pieces of hard bacon fat from that morning's breakfast. When I bit into them, they burst with flavour. I gave her a nuzzle and she whispered in my ear. 'If I have another boy, we will be naming him Vinnie, after you.'

"Was I sad to leave, Tovarisch? Well, yes. And also no. In a way, it was all about the journey, not the destination. I knew instinctively that my new home in England would be wonderful.

Together, we had a last walk around Red Square up to Saint Basil's wedding cake. Alexei asked Katya which of the multi-coloured domes was her favourite.

'The green and red dome because the red will always remind me of Vinnie, and the green is the place of my birth and Vinnie's home in the green Taiga Forest.'

Alexei smiled at his daughter's musings. Taking her by the hand, he smiled at her. 'When my posting to Moscow is over, we will go back to the green woods.'

Katya smiled back. 'Then I can have my very own Vinnie and a Dachshund!'

Alexei looked to the heavens and shook his head.

Our first stop was the vast battlefield of Borodino. There we saw the two monuments: one with a French Eagle marking Napoleon's position, another a Russian Eagle marking the spot where Marshall Kutuzov had mustered his army. Alexei bowed to both monuments, remembering all the souls who had passed away into history. Back in the car, Katya and I leant out of the window, not wanting to miss a thing as we made our way to Smolensk. As we drove, Katya's long tousled hair blowed in my face, and the cold breeze made my big ears flap.

Alexei drove towards a church that looked like a cake with mint-green icing. He called back. 'That's the Cathedral of the Blessed Virgin. We'll find a cafe near there.' In the great cathedral's shadow, Alexei and Katya ate Golubtsy, peeling off the cabbage leaves for me to eat the tasty meat inside.

On our way again, the monotonous motorway sent Katya and I into a deep sleep. When we awoke, it was dark. In the distance twinkled a city's lights. Katya rubbed her eyes. 'Where are we, Papa?'

'Approaching Minsk, where we will stay the night. I have a room booked near Independence Square. There we can take Vinnie for a walk.'

After my run, we had dinner in a little restaurant off the Square where Alexei and Katya ate borscht, a red beetroot soup topped with sour cream. The restaurant was kind enough to give me a bowl of very tasty Kolbasa sausages.

All dog tired, we made our way back to the hotel. That night I slept on Katya's bed using her feet as a pillow. In the morning before breakfast, Katya chased me around the flower beds of Independence Square.

Our next stop was the charming city of Warsaw, capital of Poland. Alexei pulled up in front of a very grand hotel. A young man in an immaculate uniform opened the rear door for Katya and was very surprised to find an orange hound bound out. In impeccable Russian, he welcomed us to Warsaw. Katya asked how he knew we were Russian. 'I'm afraid there's no secret, Miss, only your car's number plate.' The young man gave me a long stroke. 'Your dog is a Vizsla, yes?'

'Yes, he is a Hungarian breed.' The young man gave Katya a quizzical look.

'Now, why would a Hungarian dog from Russia be travelling to Poland? You know, I happen to be an aspiring writer,' he gave my ears a pull and looked me in the eyes, 'and I'm sure you have a story to tell, don't you?'

Katya smiled. 'His name is Vinnie, and his story is incredible.'

'I should like to hear it, Miss.' Caught up in his enthusiasm, he failed to notice Alexei struggling with the cases. 'I'm so sorry, sir, sometimes I forget myself.'

Alexei laughed, 'It's not a problem.' The young man picked up all the cases and carried them into the hotel, placing them with the concierge. He bowed to Katya, 'My name is Stefan. Would you and your father do me the honour of letting me show you around Warsaw tonight?' Alexei looked at Katya. Her smile said it all. Alexei thanked him, offering Stefan dinner in return.

After a quick rest in our lovely room, we met Stefan in the hotel lobby and he first showed us around the quaint Old Town Market Square. All the buildings were mismatched shapes and sizes, painted in different colours. It was like opening a fancy selection box of chocolates trying to decide which one you'd try first. Stefan led us through the old town's narrow streets. Our progress was slow as crowds of friendly people said hello to me, giving me lots of pats and everyone wanted to know my name.

From the insides of cafés came the piano music of Chopin, Szpilman and Eric Satie, mixing like a sophisticated cocktail with violin melodies from Bacewicz and Karol Szymanowski. The Polish people reminded me of my Cossack family back in the Taiga, everybody happily arguing, laughing and gesturing wildly, making jokes and telling stories. Stefan told us that Warsaw had seen enough tragedy to last a hundred lifetimes but now, like a Spring flower, the city and its people were blooming with happiness. Next, we walked onto the magnificent Royal castle, home of the old Kings of Poland. The whole building was the colour of my coat! A fiddle player ran over and pointed at me – 'Vizsla!' He played a fast, Hungarian folk song. Katya and I danced around Sigmund's Column while Stefan and Alexei clapped. Her father gave Katya a twenty Zloty note to give to the fiddle player, who thanked her, giving a little bow before he put the note under his hat, then as we walked away, he serenaded Katya by playing Salut d'Amour by Edward Elgar.

In the market Square, we had our dinner at an outdoor café. The restaurant pianist asked if anyone could play the piano. Katya put her hand up to great applause and was invited to sit next to the pianist. Together they decided to play Mozart's Piano Sonata No. 16 in C major. Many people in the square stopped to listen as the restaurant fell silent. When they had finished, all the diners and tourists erupted into applause while I barked with delight. Katya gave a small bow, then the restaurant manager came over and thanked her, presenting a big box of chocolates.

After dinner, Stefan took us to see Warsaw's most famous statue, a mermaid with a sword and shield. Stefan told us that according to legend the mermaid called Syrenka had swum up the river Vistula from the Baltic Sea to protect the people of Warsaw. Maybe I was tired and a little dreamy because, when I looked up at her, I could have sworn she turned to me and smiled. I heard her whispered words in my head telling me to have no fear for the future and a smile broke across her pretty face. Alexei called me to follow. Briefly, I looked away from her, and when I glanced back, the mermaid was once more frozen in time.

Stefan walked us back to the hotel. He shook Alexei hand's and gave me a lovely long stroke saying the sweetest things in my ear in his perfect Russian. Alexei led me to the lift, letting Stefan and Katya spend some time alone together. As the lift doors closed, we caught a glimpse of Stefan taking Katya's hand. Alexei patted me and sighed wistfully. 'I think soon I will be losing my daughter too.'

The following day, after a breakfast of cheese, cold eggs, and ham, we said goodbye to Warsaw. I felt like I was leaving an old friend behind. Back on the never-ending motorway, Alexei told us we would be stopping before Berlin at Seelow Heights, where Valentin's grand-uncle had fought. It was the last name to be etched into the blade of the sabre that Valentin had given to Sergeant Yuri.

At Seelow Heights, Katya ran around with me, throwing sticks down into the valley for me to chase. While we played, Alexei had a quiet moment. He stood looking at the view back towards Poland and Russia then, turning and dropping his head, he said Kaddish to the fallen Russian soldiers in the German onslaught, and to all those who died in that terrible battle.

On our approach to Berlin, Alexei parked in Frankfurter an der Oder. We had a long walk along the river Oder which flowed through the Park Nadodrzanski. Alexei and Katya sat down on a bench looking out over a bend in the shimmering river, quietly reflecting on all the history that had passed across all the river Oder's fine bridges. However, whereas before all our gazes were open and bright, now Alexei's seemed to be perpetually brooding.

On the autobahn again, I snuggled up on Katya's lap while she listened to music. Soon, I drifted off to sleep. She woke me up with a stroke, 'Vinnie, look!' I sat up. Katya pointed through the windscreen. In the distance, we could see a giant, silver cocktail stick pointing like a finger into the sky. Towards the tower's top glinted a giant mirrored ball and on its glass surface shone a red and yellow cross, reflecting the colours of the sunset. The cross marked our destination - soon, we would arrive in Berlin.

Our hotel was near the Brandenburg Gate. Set back in a side street of traditional German houses, the hotel had an understated elegance; each side of the steps up to the front door grew trailing grapevines. Alexei hauled the cases up the stairs. 'No bell boy here, Katya, but they do have something that I know you and Vinnie will really like.'

As Katya pushed through the door, I heard a bark not of warning but of welcome. I pushed past Alexei, knocking one of the cases out of his hand, sending it tumbling back down the steps. Running into the foyer, I saw a handsome German Pointer coming down the stairs. In one huge bound, he leapt down the final two steps. We crouched down, sizing each other up before leaping up to bump chests, chasing each other around the foyer between the hotel manager's legs, before both being shooed into the back garden. We ran in and out of the tables, surprising the diners, zooming around the apple trees. Everyone laughed, watching us run and play. My new friend's mistress called us in, 'Would you boys like something to eat?' Together we followed her, rushing into the kitchen where we shared the leftovers from lunch.

After our dinner, we were taken for an evening stroll in the beautiful Tiergarten. My new friend introduced himself as Kaiser. We had a happy nuzzle before taking off together, running in and out of the Lime trees down to the river Spree to bark at the waving tourists on the sightseeing boats.

On our return to the hotel, we curled up together in front of the fire in the bar. Kaiser told me about how he had been rescued from a farm, having been abandoned after a lifetime of work. He was such a sweet loving dog. Both of us had the right to have lost faith in humanity, but you know, Tovarisch, there are many more good people in this world who love animals.

The next day, we walked up to the Brandenburg Gate, with Alexei lingering behind, seemingly lost in another world. The huge Gate represented unity, freedom and forgiveness – although it seemed, for some, scars run deeper than for others. It felt right that I would be starting my new life here in Berlin.

When we got back to the hotel, there waiting in the lobby were a couple. Even though I didn't recognise them, I instinctively knew who they were. Katya let go of my lead. 'Vinnie!' they cried, and I went bounding over with my tail wagging, jumping on them, overwhelming them with all my Vizsla love and joy.

That evening, we had a delicious dinner in the hotel's garden where Alexei and Katya told the new couple, Ian and Helen, all about me. I climbed up onto Helen's lap. At first, she was taken aback, but Katya reassured her that I only wanted to be close to her, as it is the nature of the Vizsla breed! Kaiser sat contently on her feet and we both dozed to the sound of happy conversation and laughter.

All too soon, it was time to leave. I thought Katya would be sad, which would make me sad, but somehow, on our road trip to Berlin, she had grown up yet again. She gave me a long hug holding back her tears. However, Alexei was overcome by emotion. My friend - the tough, strong general of the police - cried like a little boy! I licked away his salty tears, and he smiled. I knew he was happy and content, after many days of brooding, knowing that he had done his duty by me and that he would be able to look Valentin in the eye to tell him Vinnie, his ever-faithful Tiger Hound, was going to his forever home. After a final hug from Katya and a nuzzle from Kaiser, I jumped into the back of Helen and Ian's car. This time going into my new life there was to be no uncertainty.

When it was lunchtime, we stopped our journey for a delicious currywurst sausage in the shadow of the magnificent double spires of Cologne cathedral. Afterwards, we walked down to the vast River Rhine, which had been used by the Romans to act as a barrier to Hunnic invasion. Ian told me we would be stopping one more time before catching the ferry to England.

We drove through southern Holland, down toards Belgium through its beautiful capital Brussels, on our way to a little town with a big name, Waterloo. The scene of the Emperor Napoleon's final defeat. Out of the car window, I saw a small mountain; on the top stood a huge black lion. Ian called back to me. 'The lion marks the spot where the Iron Duke took up his position on a ridge to face Emperor Napoleon. We have come here at Alexei's request to honour your former master, Valentin. His ancestor would have marched through here in 1814, on their way to Paris with Czar Alexander's army of Cossacks to fight Napoleon's army. There they defeated the emperor Napoleon, who was then exiled to the island of Elba. Escaping captivity, he came back to France, raising a vast army of 73,000 loyal French soldiers only to be finally defeated by Arthur Wellesley, the first Duke of Wellington and Marshall Blücher, here on the battlefield of Waterloo.'

Ian attached my lead as we walked up to the museum doors. A hoity-toity official looked down his nose at me and, with a nasal twang, spoke to Ian. 'I am afraid sir, dogs are not allowed in the museum.' Helen took my lead, telling Ian to see the museum on his own, but I hadn't come this far to be told by some snooty official that I, *Vinnie the Tiger Hound*, wasn't welcome! Pulling my lead out of Helen's hand, I ran through Snooty's legs, dodging the security guards sprinting inside the museum.

Safely inside, I ran along a corridor and skidded to a halt in front of a figure of a proud man in a green uniform. Pulled down on his head was a black bicorn hat; in its corner was the red, white and blue cockade of the French revolution. He was riding a fine grey horse. Behind me, I heard frantic shouts in French and English. The man was none other than the Emperor Napoleon himself, sitting on top of his faithful Arabian stallion Marengo. I had just enough time to look up into the Emperor's face; I swear Napoleon winked at me saying, 'Courage Mon brave, keep going up the revolution!' So, who was I to ignore the Emperor of France?

I kept running, staying a few steps in front of my pursuers. Behind me, I heard loud French curses. I slowed to look around just as Snooty reached out a hand for my trailing lead but, tripping over instead, he landed flat on his pompous face - causing more French swearing and, dare I say, a little chortle of English laughter. Round the museum I ran, leading my pursuers a merry dance, flying around cabinets full of memorabilia. I skidded to a halt in front of another horse and rider, looking up into the severe face of the Iron Duke, Arthur Wellesley, riding his beautiful chestnut Thoroughbred, Copenhagen. The duke did not wink. Instead, I heard his angry voice in my head, 'What the deuce? How dare you, Sir!' I did an about-turn away from the vexed Duke, slip-sliding on the polished floor, still managing to wrong foot my chasing pack. I high-tailed it through the outside doors leading to the little grass mountain. Round and round I raced. My pursuer tried to cut me off, but I was too quick, reaching the top before them. The view over the battlefield was spectacular, exactly the same as it had been in 1815. The magnificent lion on his plinth looked down on me and shook his shaggy mane laughing, 'Good old Vinnie, you're giving them all a run for their money!' Up the hill came a sweating, swearing Ian. I let him grab my lead. The lion winked and smiled before becoming a statue once again, looking out over the fields of Belgium towards France.

Coming out of the museum doors, there waited a very concerned Helen. On seeing Ian's sweating beaming face, she too began to see the funny side of my antics. They laughed together as behind us the museum doors slammed shut. Ian gave me a pat. 'Well Vinnie, we got to see Napoleon and Wellington for free, but your recall training starts tomorrow!'

Our next stop was the French port of Calais. There waiting at the dock was a car ferry. Once parked up, we heard the ship's foghorn blaring out. Ian led me onto the deck. Standing with my front paws on the metal rail, in the last remaining light of the day, I saw the White cliffs of Dover. The end of my 5000-mile odyssey from Siberia to England was nearly over.

"So, Tovarisch, that is my tale. If I do say so myself, it's not a bad one!"

"Vinnie, my dear friend, it's worthy of Dickens himself. Thank you for sharing with me!" Outside we heard birdsong; dawn's early light was creeping through the window. We snuggled up together into a tight ball to fall sound asleep, both dreaming of tigers in the Taiga. We slept soundly until we heard Papa coming downstairs. Together we yawned.

"Late night, boys? Come on, shake a leg, because today we are going to the beach!"

Once packed, we bundled into the back of the car, our exuberance unbounded as if going to the beach is the best thing ever – which, in a way, it is! But after our initial burst of Vizsla excitement, our heads became heavy, and we curled up together on the back seat to fall into a deep sleep. I awoke to the car window being wound down. I sniffed the air. My acute sense of smell picked out the familiar odour of salt and seaweed. Nudging Vinnie awake, even though we were still five miles from the beach, our noses were already out at sea, and together we inhaled deep breaths of salty air.

Through the level crossing gates into Frinton on Sea, we couldn't contain our enthusiasm, jumping on Papa as he tried to park the car, demanding to be let out. After what seemed like an age, the car door finally opened. "Come on, Vinnie," Czar barked, "I know the way." Straight across the grassy greensward and down the steep hill. Hooray, the tide was going out! Past the colourful beach huts, down the wooden steps, and finally onto the warm sand. We raced down to the sea. Vinnie bounced around running in and out of the salty water, jumping the white horses. Two golden retrievers bounded up to play. We all chased round and round, jumping breakwaters and scaring the seagulls fighting over seaweed. Out at sea floated a white raft. The four of us swam for all we were worth to reach the bobbing raft first. Scrambling on board, we took in the happy view back towards Frinton: the multi-coloured beach huts, kids building sandcastles and flying kites, plus the smell of sausages frying tickled our taste buds.

Diving off the raft, we all swam to shore for a shake, blinking out the salty water. Vinnie went to investigate one of the old wooden breakwaters. Exploring, he sniffed about, poking his nose where it wasn't wanted. Suddenly, he ran backwards, yelping. There, pinching his soft nose with its pincer, hung a large green Common crab. Vinnie shook his head until the crab released its vice-like grip, dropping onto the beach and scuttling away to bury itself back in the sand, until only its two stalky eyes remained. I couldn't help but laugh. "You could have warned me, Tovarisch, that crab's nippers brought tears to my eyes!" Walking around the breakwater, Vinnie eyed the hidden crab with new respect.

Running along the beach, we made our way to Walton on the Naze, jumping breakwaters, playing with other dogs and running in and out of the sea. When we got to Walton, Papa bought us both two tasty sausages, which we wolfed down, eyed by a flock of hungry seagulls.

The following day it poured with rain. Wearing our coats, we watched Papa feeding and brushing the ponies, preparing for the next day when we would be trekking through Epping Forest.

Up early the next morning, we watched the two sleepy ponies enthusiastically run up the trailer ramp. Closing the door behind them, we were on our way. As soon as we came off the motorway, I knew exactly where we were, as we passed the ancient oak and beech trees. Papa parked in a clearing. I saw Gill, Enza's rider, waiting by her car. On seeing Vinnie and me, she crouched down; with our tails wagging, we jumped on her, covering her clean clothes with muddy footprints. Papa and Gill tacked up the horses. Vinnie whispered to me, putting his paw on my shoulder, "You know, Tovarisch, I never thought I would ever follow horses again, so I must thank your master." Vinnie gave Papa's hand a contented nuzzle, in return for a stroke. Feeling slightly jealous, I bounded over to Papa for a fuss too.

Gill and Papa mounted up. I led, knowing the way down towards Fairmead Bottom. Vinnie and I darted in and out of the trees, chasing innumerable squirrels up the old oaks, watching them disappear up tree trunks before darting into the safety of old woodpecker holes. I found a long stick to carry proudly through the trees. Vinnie decided it was his, grabbing it, we wrestled, trying to wrench it away from each other's jaws.

When we came to a long stretch of grass, Papa and Gill pushed the two ponies into a gallop. Dropping his end of the stick, Vinnie charged off in front to lead the way. His legs whirled away so fast I thought he would take off and fly. At the end of the field, he sat down, panting heavily, his amber eyes wide with joy.

We had a cooling drink in a forest stream before going deeper into the woods. We trotted together in and out of the dense holly, hunting around in the fallen leaves, digging under rotting logs and finding many intriguingly wild smells. Emerging onto a long stretch of grassland, the horses' ears pricked forward, knowing where they were, wanting to gallop. Leaping forward, bucking with excitement, I knew the way, so I led with Vinnie close at my side, our ears flying in the wind, the exciting sound of the horses' hooves thundered behind us.

The grassland opened up to reveal Chingford Plain. The air overhead buzzed with model aircrafts, and children flying kites and playing hide and seek. The horses were both wide-eyed and alert, ready to spook away from a possible attack from marauding plastic bags. In the middle of the plain calmly stood a herd of brown and white Longhorn cattle. Disinterested, they slowly raised their heads, watching us canter past. Crossing the brook, the horses galloped hard up the hill towards the Tudor splendour of the Queen Elizabeth Hunting Lodge. Gill and Papa dismounted at Butlers Retreat Café for a hot chocolate. Vinnie and I lay down, looking out at the view over the plains, watching other dogs charging happily through the long grass. It was good to see Vinnie enjoying his holiday, so happy and content.

Crossing Rangers Road, we made our way towards Warren Hill - the fastest gallop in Epping Forest. Starting at the bottom of the hill, by the old lightning tree, the horses slowly moved off in formation, like Czar Alexander's Cossack cavalry. The snorting horses advanced up the hill, moving first into a slow trot, which became a canter. Papa and Gill let the horses have their heads as the two mares galloped joyously forward, tearing up the hill. Snorting, Enza swerved out in front, so that Lolo, the faster horse, couldn't overtake her. "Shall we race too, Tovarisch?"

"Let's do it, Vinnie, first one to the ancient oak?" Leaping straight into a gallop, we shot up the hill, accelerating hard, swerving into each other, bumping and ramming, trying to knock one or the other off our stride. Halfway up the hill, Vinnie gave me a hard sideswipe causing me to stumble, tumbling onto the grass. I lay still. Vinnie rushed over all concerned, "Tovarisch, are you hurt?" I sprung up, galloping off. "Fooled you, loser!" Leaving the seething Vinnie to eat my dust, I reached the oak tree first, followed by a puffing Vinnie. "Very cheeky, Tovarisch," he said, giving me a friendly nip for my impudence.

Crossing the Epping Forest New Road, we followed the forest tracks passing Strawberry Hill Pond, over the Earl's Path, before going back into the forest. Gill and Papa walked the horses on a long rein, giving me and Vinnie time to sniff around between the trees. Suddenly Vinnie stopped and pointed. I looked to see what his sharp eyes had spotted and there in the trees, blending in perfectly, were a herd of Fallow deer. Deer are always fascinated by horse and rider as if they are some sort of mythical beast. The deer stared; we stared back. Vinnie ran forward a few steps, the herd of deer stood their ground. Vinnie suddenly stopped. A stag moved out in front of the herd to protect his does. He watched us, seemingly unconcerned, his proud head held high topped with antlers like two small trees – magnificent! We heard Papa quietly ask us to sit. Obediently we sat down. The stag dropped his head and turned, followed by his herd with their white tails bobbing. Gradually they disappeared into the cover of the holly trees. The horses, slightly spooked by the deer, wanted to canter off in the opposite direction. After a minute or so, they became calm again. Walking on, we followed the path the deer had taken up the hill towards the Lost Pond.

We left the horses to rest. Vinnie ran off on a scent. I followed close on his heels as he raced across the Green Ride into Loughton camp, a pre-Roman Iron age fort. Vinnie galloped on as if he knew the way; something seemed to be drawing him to that ancient, magical place. On the edge of the camp, Vinnie stopped. There, in the middle between the tall, grey beech trees, sat three Vizslas: two males, and a smaller female. I went to run towards them, but Vinnie checked me. "Tovarisch, please wait here." Somehow, I knew not to argue, as Vinnie trotted towards them. The biggest of the hounds left his two companions and walked towards Vinnie, his head down. The two dogs stalked around each other growling, baring their teeth, suddenly lunging forward to fight. They battled, tumbling through the leaves and undergrowth, grappling the other, kicking and snapping. A trial of strength ensued.

The two other Vizsla looked on, smiling knowingly as if they had seen it all before. Vinnie's opponent, marked with old battle scars, launched another vicious attack, throwing poor Vinnie to the ground. My heart was in my mouth and my hackles rose - wanting to help, but Vinnie didn't need my help. Despite his years, he side-stepped the bigger Vizsla with great agility, kicking him hard in the chest, sending him sprawling. Springing up together, the two dogs eyed each other.

Suddenly, like clouds parting to reveal the sun, both dogs relaxed and bumped chests. Laughing, they embraced, sat down, began talking to each other. I saw Vinnie shaking his head. Looking back, he indicated to me as the other dog looked over Vinnie's shoulder, giving me an angry look. I could see he was beginning to lose his temper with Vinnie, getting very angry. Vinnie shook his head defiantly; the bigger dog rose to his full height, his hackles now prominently raised. I thought he and Vinnie were going to fight again. The pretty female walked forward, coming between them, talking to Vinnie and the other dog in turn. Vinnie bowed to her, as did the other dog but more grudgingly, then the third Vizsla, who looked like Vinnie, joined them. Finally, all four hounds came together as one, entwining necks, saying their fond goodbyes. Vinnie came trotting back towards me. The three Vizslas watched the departing Vinnie, his head held high and tail wagging. Shaking their heads, they moved off back into the trees. Vinnie stopped and turned, watching them disappear into the holly, beech and oak. I trotted up to Vinnie, together we stared at the fast-disappearing Vizslas. "Ahhh, Tovarisch, were you worried?" Vinnie asked.

"No... well, yes... slightly, Vinnie. I'm just confused. Who were they?"

"Well, Tovarisch, the smaller dog is my brother Istvan, the beautiful female is Catherine my mate, the big narky dog is Igor the Bold."

"Really? Why were they here?"

"They came to tell me that my life here is over and it's time for me to join them, to fly with the spirit pack, but I said NO! - I'm not going. I'm enjoying my holiday with my new Tovarisch too much. That's why Igor got angry, but my beautiful Catherine calmed him down. Igor called me arrogant – me, Tovarisch, arrogant? How dare he?" Vinnie winked, "I will let them know when I'm good and ready to go, not the other way around!"

From the edge of Loughton Camp, we heard Papa calling. When we appeared out of trees, we got lots of praise from Papa and Gill. We barked with delight, running in and out of the horses' legs with Vinnie and I leading, and we headed off down the Green Ride.

The following day we lay together in the garden, lazily watching a robin, his breast the same colour as our coats. Vinnie told me more about his life in the Taiga: how you could stand on a high hill, turn a full circle, and see nothing but larch forest for as far as the eye could see. But he also told me the Siberian wilderness was under threat from unscrupulous loggers cutting down vast swathes of ancient Taiga Forest, trees hundreds of years old sawn up by the timber mills in the west, destroying the tigers, bears' and wolves' natural habitat. With the help of Cossacks and the other people of Siberia, the authorities were doing their best to catch these unscrupulous men whose eyes are only filled with rouble and dollar signs.

The next morning, we jumped in the car again to drive to the pretty village of Dedham in Suffolk, so picturesque it had been painted by three of the most famous British artists: John Constable, Thomas Gainsborough and Alfred Munnings. Papa led us to a boathouse on the river Stour. Vinnie looked at the rowing boats with deep suspicion. "Tovarisch, I have never been in such a craft. Is it safe?"

"Safe, Vinnie? You're joking! Much safer than standing up to a wild tiger!"

"Yes, that's true Tovarisch, your point is well made." Papa climbed into the boat first then helped the nervous leg-flailing Vinnie aboard. I jumped smartly in. Now it was my turn to give Vinnie a smug wink. Together we sat up in the prow of the boat. While Papa rowed, we took in the life of the river. Looking down into the crystal-clear water, we watched shoals of minnows darting like silver arrows, swans moving serenely amongst dipping and diving ducks. Papa rowed under trailing branches of the crack willow trees. until he got the boat tangled up in a mass of dangling weeping willow, to the indignation of a family of moorhens. On the grassy banks, families enjoying their picnics waving at our happy passing.

As we rounded a bend in the river, there sitting on a log gnawing at a twig of sweet willow was a furry brown water rat. Vinnie, who had until that moment sat calmly, suddenly became alert. Leaping out of the boat, he belly-flopped into the river with an almighty splash - drenching Papa. Vinnie paddled like fury. I leant over the side of the boat, barking furiously. Having seen all manner of dogs before, the water rat looked nonplussed; only when Vinnie was scrambling frantically through the cloying mud, did the rat make his way casually back to his hole in the riverbank. Clambering up the bank, Vinnie stood on the grass, defeated but proud, shaking himself dry. He waited until Papa rowed the boat to the bank. Now giving the impression of being an old river dog, he jumped straight back in, taking his place beside me. "Tovarisch, if only I could have swum faster. I would have had him."

"Yes Vinnie, of course you would," I said, massaging his ego. I looked at Vinnie, his eyes never leaving the water rat's hole until it disappeared behind the bulrushes. He turned to me and gave me a wink - I loved my deluded friend.

Papa rowed on. Further up, the river widened and there in front of us was the setting for one of the most famous scenes in the world of art, John Constable's painting, The Haywain. Prominent in the painting is Willy Lott's cottage and neither the cottage nor the river Stour had changed since John Constable first opened-up his paint box in 1821. Papa unshipped the oars and lay back, letting the boat drift. We hung our paws over the side, feeling the cool water eddying around them. Vinnie looked about, watching the shimmering green and orange dragonflies dancing. A blue kingfisher dived like an arrow catching a minnow before streaking away across the water's surface. "Tovarisch, this is a very beautiful place, the water tastes as sweet as a Siberian stream, but is much warmer. Would you join me in a swim?"

"Vinnie, my friend, it would be rude not to." Climbing onto the side of the boat, we both dived in together, sending up a double fountain of water, soaking poor Papa again. He didn't seem to mind. Only a pair of Mallard ducks flew up in consternation. So clear was the water that we could see each

other's legs paddling away. Climbing onto the bank, we had a big shake, then followed Papa as he rowed the boat back upstream. Vinnie and I ran along the grassy bank in and out of the reed beds, jumping over fallen willow trees, making our way back towards the distant spire of Dedham Church.

Our lovely day was completed at the Sun Inn on Dedham High Street, where Papa treated us both to sausage and mash, while he relaxed in an armchair. Dog tired, we dozed off in front of the fireplace. All too soon, our holiday would be coming to an end; Vinnie's people Ian and Helen would be arriving at lunchtime the following day.

Early the next day, on our morning walk, we made our way to Acorn Wood. We sat on a log just watching and listening to the wood's wildlife; the hammer of the woodpecker heard but unseen. A suspicious vixen peaked out of her den, her cubs scrabbling behind her, desperate to leave their underground home. Unnoticed, we sat stock still, watching the cubs playing in the broken sunlight, which filtered through the oak leaves. We left our nemesis, the squirrels, undisturbed to gather and bury their nuts, watching them chase each other up and down the branches of the trees. Soon nature accepted our presence, and its wild world opened up in front of us. Vinnie chatted away happily, but I was quiet and reflective. Vinnie sensed my mood. "Tovarisch, not so sad. We will see each other again soon. Remember, you are the Czar, and like Czar Peter the Great and Czarina Catherine, soon you will go on and do something great to make a difference to the lives of other less fortunate dogs, leaving home to go on your own odyssey. Then, you will be known as the Great Red Czar! Be in no doubt, Tovarisch, I will join you on your journey and be there at your side to guide you through our second big adventure together."

Dasvidaniya Czar

ABOUT THE AUTHOR

Stephen was born and raised in the Epping Forest area, brought up by his grandparents after being abandoned by his mother. Due to his grandparents being elderly, he was sent to boarding school aged six. He struggled at school due to severe dyslexia, which wasn't fully recognised at the time. It was only after learning to ride horses that he discovered a life-long passion, becoming a proficient show jumper and then working as a Polo player. Animals subsequently played a leading role in Stephen's life, but, after a bad fall, it was time to give up Polo and pursue something completely different. Here entered the world of dogs, and especially the desire to help those who had suffered abuse or been abandoned. Following six months of hard training, Stephen began a charity walk around the UK coastline with his dog, Czar.

They started at Brighton Pier, heading west. The idea was mainly to wild camp, and Stephen carried a forty kilogram rucksack containing everything for him and Czar to camp under the stars. They spent 24 hours a day together, allowing Stephen to get a greater understanding of how dog's interact and to observe their psychology.

Due to the Covid-19 pandemic, the trip had to be brought to a premature end. Coming back into a locked-down world was a huge challenge: no work was available, and he had nowhere to live. Even the few homeless organisations he came across were not able to accept dogs. As a consequence, he ended up living in a trailer on a field, alongside Czar and two horses. With nightly temperatures sometimes plunging to minus 8 degrees, it was a struggle just to survive. And that's when Stephen turned to writing. The encouragement came from a lady called Jane Russell, who had personally rescued three Pointer hounds. She was really moved by Stephen's journey, and told him it reminded her of a book called The Salt Path.

Stephen began to write what was to become a trilogy of books. The first, Vinnie's Odyssey, was inspired by a visit of a special Vizsla dog of the same name. Vinnie had been rescued but nothing was known of his history; he had scars and burn marks all across his body. Amazingly, whatever he had gone through, Vinnie still had a loving nature. Czar and Vinnie immediately became best friends, enjoying their holiday together, and it inspired Stephen to open a sanctuary for abandoned and abused dogs, for which profits of this book will go towards.

Vinnie and Czar will return in

THE DIARIES
OF A
CZAR
CZAR'S ODYSSEY